TALES OF BANARAS
The Flowing Ganges

HINDOO TEMPLE, BENARES

TALES OF BANARAS
The Flowing Ganges

The Life and Lore of India's
Sacred City on the Ganges

Translated from the original Hindi of Rudra Kashikey,
pen name of Shiv Prasad Mishra
by

Paul R. Golding
with
Virendra Singh

BOOK FAITH INDIA
Delhi

TALES OF BANARAS
The Flowing Ganges

Published by
BOOK FAITH INDIA
414-416 Express Tower, Azadpur Commercial Complex
Delhi, India 110 033

Distributed by
PILGRIMS BOOK HOUSE
P.O. Box 3872, Kathmandu, Nepal
P.O. Box 38, Varanasi, India
Fax 977-1-424943. E-mail: info@pilgrims.wlink.com.np

 Copyediting and Typesetting by John Snyder Jr.

Editing by Daniel Haber, Sian Pritchard-Jones and Bob Gibbons

Cover Design by Sherap Sherpa - Pilgrims Red House Business Center

ISBN 81-7303-054-5

1st English Edition
Translated with permission from the Hindi text *Bahati Ganga*
Copyright © 1997 Paul R. Golding

Printed in New Delhi, India by Surya Print Process

Table of Contents

Illustrations

Acknowledgements

One seldom hears the words "thank you" in India, as if the utterance of such gratitude detracts from the act of generosity that produces it. Without any such intent, however, I would like to acknowledge with thanks the help I received from several people in both Banaras and Washington in the course of translating and annotating this book. First and foremost, I feel tremendous gratitude to Virendra Singh of the University of Wisconsin Year in India program for his wonderful introduction to India and Hindi and for his extensive help with all aspects of this book. Thanks also to Mahant Veer Bhadra Mishra of the Sanket Mochan Temple and Banaras Hindu University for his many comments, repeated and generous hospitality, and warm support; to Dr. Bhanu Shankar Mehta for sharing his experience with and knowledge of Banaras' folk life; to the author's children, Avanindra, Arvinda, and Jyotsana Mishra and Premlata Pandey, for permission to translate and publish their father's work; to Mark Dyczkowski, Rana P.B. Singh, and Manon LaFleur for their help and support while in Banaras. In Washington, my gratitude goes to a transplanted Banarasi, Shaligram Shukla of Georgetown University, for help with many of the details of the Hindi translation, and to Abbie Ziffren of George Washington University for editorial assistance, for her interest in translation of Indian literature generally, and for help with this particular one. Finally, I would like to thank Susan Foster for her many helpful suggestions and support in this effort.

Introduction

This collection of tales is the book that most literary-minded citizens of Banaras mention when asked to recommend a modern work of fiction about their sacred city. The book's Hindi title, *Bahati Ganga*, means "the flowing Ganges," and as this river, which flows along one side of the city, is the source of spiritual and material richness to the people of India, so too this book is a source of richness in Banaras lore—its history, spiritual life, lifestyles, and prejudices.

The city where these stories are set offers its residents and visitors many different ways to enjoy its charms. Like the hundreds of thousands of Hindus who come to the city every year, one may go on a pilgrimage, visit the important temples in the city, descend the wide, long steps at the five most important riverside ghats to bathe in the Ganges, and catch sight of Lord Shiva's image at the main Vishvanath temple. One may sit in one of the city's hundreds of tea stalls and observe the frenetic energy of the streets and lanes—the rickshaw traffic jams, the shrouded dead bodies being carried to cremation grounds, the crowds of men gathered at the neighborhood *pan* shop gossiping, with heads tilted backwards so as not to stain their clothing with the red betelnut mixture in their mouths. Or one may go to the "other side," the far shore of the Ganges, grind some *bhang* (hashish), wash one's clothes, cook a meal over cow dung cakes, and have a traditional Banarasi good time.

One can experience Banaras in these and other ways, but for me there has also been this book, which at some early point in the work of translating became my personal guide to the city. I have travelled with it through the city, and back and forth in time, as well. It has helped me stop the frantic pace of the life of Banaras, concentrate on one feature at a time and glimpse the thoughts of Banarasis, to understand better what they feel and how they experience their world.

How most Banarasis see their world begins, I believe, with accepting the presence of the gods and the magic truth of myth. In this regard, Banarasis often tell a popular story, recorded perhaps a thousand years ago, but probably much older, about how the city became populated with so many gods and what price their presence exacts. The story is told in detail elsewhere[1] but, in brief, it begins with the world on the verge of destruction. The creator Brahma, looking about for someone to rule, found only King Ripunjaya, retired in Banaras practicing asceticism. The king agreed to accept the responsibility of restoring order to the world on one condition: the gods must leave Banaras and return to heaven. Ripunjaya, or Divodasa as he eventually came to be called, established a perfect government on earth and ruled for many years. Seeing this, and wishing to return to their beloved Banaras after some time had passed, the gods, especially Shiva, became jealous and started to plot the king's downfall. They sneaked back into the city and, using stealth and deception, eventually succeeded in getting rid of the king. The gods returned, perfection disappeared, and Banaras again became filled with the rich chaos of the sacred dimension of life.

[1] Diana L. Eck, *Banaras; City of Light*, Alfred A. Knopf, New York, 1982, pp. 146-57.

In places where people strongly feel this sacred dimension of life, everything is affected by and included in it. I believe the implications of this reality are far reaching in these stories. Not only are they filled with explicit references to the gods—from the opening invocation to Ganesh, through Hanuman, Shiva and Vishnu and into the ghost-world of the ancestors, but also, the very style of their narration is rooted in this world view, and hence reflects the sacred as well. From the unambiguous, and sometimes idealized, characters, to plot structures that emphasize external action and use the technique of framing one story within the context of another, I find myself often recalling the characters and style of the great Hindu epics, the *Ramayana* and the *Mahabharata*. As these epics come out of an aesthetic tradition whose goal has been to provide their audience an intimate experience with the divine through the emotional experience of character and plot, so I believe this was an objective of the author of these stories. Here, however, instead of dealing with the monumental themes of the epics, his stories abound with the themes and details of everyday Banaras life and popular history, which to the city's citizens are almost as full of the numinous as the great gods and goddesses.

The way the sacred makes itself felt in these stories also has to do with the way society is reflected. When we read these stories, we are transported to a society governed by tradition, where shared principles of propriety play a dominant role. These principles, the fabric of social values, come from the religious core of India. This is reflected, for example, in the place of the caste system or beliefs about the roles of men and women in society or rules of right behavior. In this regard, I sometimes wonder if the author's practice of having main characters appear as minor characters in prior stories is his way of emphasizing the communal, close-knit, and traditional nature of the society he writes about.

One implication of entering, by means of these stories, such a traditional society in which shared values and experience dominate is that a great deal of psychological, physical and other descriptive material is left out or is alluded to only briefly. Because the writer shares his original Banaras audience's experiences and values, a lot of background information only requires the briefest mention to bring it into the reader's focus. However, the foreign audience of this translation may not be so fortunate. For this reason, brief story introductions, glossaries, and postscript notes at the end of the stories fill in for the reader's possible lack of familiarity with the Banaras environment.

Banaras History to the Eighteenth Century

In addition to the sacred in these stories, there is also the profane, and this includes the historical events used as backdrops to the tales below. These historical backgrounds portray most of the important past of Banaras from the early eighteenth century until the time of independence from Britain in 1947. Banarasis love their city's history, so it is fitting that a fictionalized account of it should be so popular. From this history, they derive the tremendous pride of place for which they are renowned. Not only is Banaras today an important city of over a million people, but the place where death brings liberation is also considered a kind of matrix of north Indian culture and civilization—for it was in Banaras that Shiva is said to have had Vishnu create the world, and it was to Banaras that the Buddha came to preach his first sermon. It was also in Banaras that some of the great saints of the Jains were born. In Banaras one can find a counterpart for almost all the important mythological events of India's past.

These stories, which pick up this history beginning in the eighteenth century, take the reader into the midst of an historical tale that starts long before that time. Just as the dry Ganges reveals layers to the ghats when the river is low that a visitor cannot see in the high water of the rainy season, so these stories are based on earlier layers of Banaras' history that may not be immediately visible. Hence, a brief summary of that history may help the reader to appreciate Banaras' past more fully.

The earliest mention of Banaras appears in Sanskrit texts, the surviving versions of which were written centuries later than the events they describe. These texts which mention "Kashi"—another term for Banaras—include some of the most important sources of Hinduism and Buddhism, including the above-mentioned epics the *Ramayana* and the *Mahabharata*, some of the earlier Vedic literature, and the later-written *Puranas*, as well as the Jataka tales of the Buddha.[1] In spite of doubts raised about the accuracy of the claims made in these sources, historians know from them that a Kingdom of Kashi was among the important kingdoms of the middle Ganges plain in the first half of the first millennium B.C.[2] Around 800-600 B.C. this kingdom dominated the region, but by about 600 B.C. it came under the influence of the Kingdom of Magadha based in today's Bihar State.[3]

The capital of Kashi was Varanasi—the official name of Banaras today. This Varanasi was probably an important crossroads. Though we cannot be certain that the ancient city is the same as the one of today, the geographical situation of the current Varanasi suggests an importance and centrality to this spot. It is believed that a path, road, or highway—today known as the Grand Trunk Road—has passed through Banaras for millennia connecting the northwest of India with the southeastern population centers in Bihar, Bengal, and Orissa. Also, the Ganges, which normally flows southeastward, abruptly turns north before it reaches Banaras, creating a north-south barrier in the middle of the Ganges Basin. Undoubtedly, this contributed to Banaras' reputation as a *tirtha*, which on the one hand literally means a crossing, but on the other, figuratively, means a place where one's spirit may cross into another reality (that is to say, a sacred place). Perched loftily on three hills overlooking the river, the site must have always been impressive:

---

[1] Chand, Moti, *Kashi Ka Itihas*, Vishvavidyalay Prakashan, Varanasi, 1985, pp. 19-30.

[2] Sukul, Kuber Nath, *Varanasi Down the Ages*, Publisher: Prof. Kameshwar Nath Sukul, Rajendra Nagar, Patna, pp. 1-11.

[3] Pandey, Rajendra, *Kasi Through the Ages*, Sundeep Prakashan, Delhi, 1979, pp.29-43.

a crossroads and a river crossing, a place for commerce in trade and ideas—as well as for more clearly transcendental activities.

In addition to textual evidence, excavations carried out in the northern part of the city during the 1940s and 1960s, in what today is called the Raj Ghat Plateau (exactly where the Grand Trunk Road crosses the Ganges via the Malviya Bridge), have uncovered signs of human habitation dating back at least to the ninth century B.C.

That this Kashi Kingdom and its center, Varanasi, was an important place, conferring some special sacred legitimacy on both events and people, can perhaps be inferred from the fact that the Buddha in the fourth century B.C. after his enlightenment in Gaya to the east came to a place near Banaras to seek his first disciples and start preaching the middle way. This has made Banaras, or more precisely Sarnath—the "deer forest" five miles to the north, an important pilgrimage center for Buddhists. Similarly, Jains have established a temple to commemorate the birth of one of their twenty-four *Jinas* in southern Banaras. In fact, Jains hold that four *Jinas*, or "victorious ones," have been born in Banaras.

The following centuries saw the arrival, as well as the departure, of the first empires of India: the Mauryas (321 B.C.–185 B.C.) and the Guptas (A.D. 319 –A.D. 467). Though Banaras was no longer the capital, the city became renowned during this period as an educational center where young men of the upper castes, especially Brahmins, could come and study classical religious texts under the authority of a guru.

This was also a time when the local, pre-Aryan deities closely associated with nature were evolving and becoming absorbed into the great gods and goddesses of the Hindu pantheon that we see today. Especially notable in this regard was the development of Vishnu and Shiva as the two overarching deities of Hindu devotion, an importance which appears in the stories with characters described as a Vaishnava or a Shaivaite. During this time (about A.D. 500), the devotional emphasis of the Vedas on elaborate sacrifices carried out by a handful of designated priests gave way to the more personal relationship between

xiv

devotee and divine that came to be called *bhakti*, the way to salvation through loving devotion to the Divine Person.[1]

From the demise of the Guptas at the end of the fifth century to the rise of the Gahadavalas in the early eleventh century, Banaras seems to have fallen under the reign of several neighboring kingdoms for short periods of time. The changes at the top of the ruling structures at this time appear to have had little effect on daily life; and from the descriptions of foreign travelers, Banaras was a prosperous city with a very rich religious life. One Chinese visitor, Hiuen Tsiang, for example, found over 100 Hindu temples and at least 10,000 followers, most of whom appear to have been dedicated to the worship of Shiva—some completely tonsured, others with long, matted locks of hair, naked or ash covered. He also described a large and impressive 100-foot *lingam* made of bronze in one temple. Sarnath was still a major center for Buddhists, and reports of the period show the increasing influence of tantric and shaivaite ideas there.[2]

Banaras' golden age before the dark years of Muslim rule came in the early eleventh century when the first kingdom since the Kashi Kingdom of 600 B.C. was centered in Banaras. From reports of the time, the Gahadavalas were capable and tolerant rulers under whom Banaras flourished. They were receptive to Buddhist, Shaivite, and Vaishnava influence and were generous in their patronage to religious institutions. They also contributed to the construction of a number of new lavish temples in Banaras. They were not very good, however, about keeping the northwest frontier protected against invaders whose influences were eventually to change drastically the face of Banaras.

The first Muslim invasions into India occurred in the early 1000s when Mahmud Ghazi, the son of a Turkish nobleman, almost annually raided northwest Indian temple towns from his base in Afghanistan, searching for gold. In the process, he destroyed the idols and religious institutions of the infidels he found there. These early raids do not ap-

---

[1] For a more elaborate description of this process, see Eck, Diana, *Op. Cit.*, pp. 51-54, 60-62.
[2] Chand, Moti, *Op. Cit.*, pp. 98-101.

XV

pear to have gone as far east as Banaras. However, this situation changed with the arrival of Muhammad Ghuri, who together with other Turks and Afghans established the Delhi Sultanate in 1206. The fifteen years before these momentous events in Delhi witnessed the looting and destruction of many of Banaras' temples and the flight of some of Banaras' Brahmin religious establishment to South India for refuge. In general, the arrival of Muslim rule threw Banaras into a long bleak period quite different from the preceding century of the Gahadavalas. The city was ruled over by other east Indian principalities located in such places as Jaunpur and Ghazipur and connected to the Sultan in Delhi via the aristocratic confederation that then loosely held north India together.

The destruction of temples referred to above occurred several times over the next five hundred years; but, in spite of occasional periods of intolerance and the relative obscurity to which Banaras was confined, these were still important years in the religious development of the city. From about A.D. 1200 to A.D. 1500, some of the most important of the Banaras *Mahatmyas* were written. These Sanskrit language texts contain descriptions of Banaras' ritual geography, its mythical past, the benefits that accrue to visitors, and the manners in which pilgrimage, worship, and bathing should be observed. Furthermore, in contrast to the traditional sacred center of Banaras that was being extolled in the *Mahatmyas* at this time, important developments were also taking place in popular devotion in the city introduced by three of Banaras' more extraordinary sons. One was Ramananda (about 1400) who was a *sannyasi*, a renouncer, who taught that fervent worship of Lord Ram leads to release from the cycle of rebirth. Ramananda broke from tradition by extolling the equality of all men and the evils of caste. He is supposed to have included among his disciples both women and untouchables, including Ravi Das, the great poet of the leather worker caste, whose birthday nowadays is celebrated in Banaras with demonstrations by the city's low caste community. In addition to Ramanand and Ravi Das, there was also Kabir (1440-1518), the illegitimate son of a Brahmin, raised by Julahas, a low caste of Muslim weavers converted from Hinduism. He showed a caustic irreverence for the tenets of all established religion, emphasizing instead an individual's relationship with God and a concomitant belief in social equality.

In 1525 a new, more energetic Muslim power took over Delhi—the Moghuls. From the accession to power of the first Moghul emperor, Babur, until the early 1700s, Moghul creativity and energy controlled most of north India. Some of the Moghul emperors, most notably Akbar, were known for their tolerance and sympathy for Hinduism, but others, especially Aurangzeb, are infamous even to the present day for the opposite tendency. Indeed, the fact that no temple standing in Banaras today can be dated before the eighteenth century seems to be attributable in large measure to Aurangzeb's anti-Hindu fervor. In Banaras, two prominent mosques today stand on spots where the most spectacular Shiva and Vishnu temples once had been. Both mosques today are referred to as "Aurangzeb's Mosques" by the Hindu population.

Gradually, the Moghul empire broke up, and Banaras fell to the successor state located in today's Lucknow. This brings us to the early eighteenth century and to the events of these stories: the establishment of the Hindu Rajah in 1739, the arrival of the British, the folk heroes and folk life of the nineteenth century, the beginning of the movement for independence, and the continuing communal tension between Hindus and Muslims.

About the Author of these Stories

In addition to faith, custom, and history, these stories are also notable for their tragedy and sadness, and for the prominent place given to outsiders and misfit characters—to prostitutes, thugs, and abandoned wives. This literary manifestation of alienation, anger, and rebellion mirrors what acquaintances of the author remember of him, and what is conveyed by the author's pen name, "Rudra Kashikey." Rudra literally means "Howler," and is the earliest recorded name for the god Shiva. In the oldest sources of the Hindu tradition, the Vedas, Rudra (Shiva) is an angry god, one to be feared, an outsider to human society who lives apart with the animals, the one who looks after the impure aspects of the sacrifice.

The writer's pen name was given to him when he was a young man, according to his elder son, Lal. One day when a number of famous Hindi writers of Banaras were visiting Rudra's father, one guest remarked that the host's son resembled Lord Shiva's Rudra aspect in his angry, rebellious personality. The name stuck when Premchand, one of the writers present and perhaps the greatest and most famous writer in modern Hindi, agreed. The "Kashikey" at the end of his name is an honorific, a title which literally means that he is of Kashi, or Banaras, as, indeed, is Lord Shiva.

Rudra was born in 1911 and died in 1970. The house where he was born, where he lived most of his life, and where he died, is still the family house, located in an old, densely packed quarter of the city, and occupied now by the author's two sons, Lal and Gopal. The two-storey stone structure, built like most large Banarasi houses around a courtyard, faces a narrow busy lane, named (and famed) after a popular Banarasi snack, *kachauri*. From here to Banaras' main Vishvanath Temple near Chauk, in the heart of the city, one only has to walk a few minutes through the city's narrow lanes.

Rudra attended the prominent English schools of his day in Banaras, receiving an MA from Banaras Hindu University and a teaching degree from the Teacher's College. He worked for about twelve years as a teacher, school inspector, and journalist until he was appointed a lecturer at Banaras Hindu University in 1951.

Rudra's father and maternal grandfather were well-known *purohits tirtha*—hereditary pilgrimage priests who look after the spiritual and material needs of their pilgrim clients—providing room and board and seeing to their proper escort around the city to visit necessary religious places and perform appropriate ceremonies. Rudra's upbringing in the house of a prominent *tirtha purohit* must have influenced his life, and his stories in two areas for which Banarasi *tirtha purohits* are renowned. One is the classical "sacred center" Banaras of pilgrimages, the city of Shiva where death brings liberation. This is the Banaras whose praises are sung in the Sanskrit *Mahatmyas* mentioned above. The other aspect of Banaras to which Rudra must have been fully exposed as the son of an important *tirtha purohit* is the more shadowy side of the pilgrimage business, characterized by violent competition among rival groups of religious functionaries struggling to maintain their share of the pilgrim traffic. In this connection, Rudra's acquaintances often tell how his father would never leave the family compound unless escorted by a troop of well-armed *gundas* or thug bodyguards.

This dark side of the more down-to-earth Banaras has its lighter side as well; and this is captured in the concept of *musti*, the laid-back, easy-going attitude toward life that Banarasis are proud. The city where liberation from future rebirth is all but certain seems also to have engendered an appreciation for the good things of this life: poetry, music, idle hours in tea shops, outings to take *pan* and *bhang* and enjoy the fresh air, and raucous popular celebrations. These two aspects of Banaras folk culture—thuggery and musti—permeate these stories, as they must have permeated Rudra's life.

More generally influencing Rudra was the rich literary tradition of his city. Banaras has always been a literary center. Kabir and Ravi Das have already been mentioned, but one should also note that the Brahmin poet and popularizer of the *Ramayana*, Tulsi Das, was, for a time in his life, a Banarasi. The works of these three men are embedded in the soul of North India, and they can be quoted, and indeed are quoted, by people from all strata of Indian society even today. As Rudra's stories are carriers of the Banaras tradition, the implicit and at times explicit influence of these three men is very strong. In addition, modern Hindi India owes much to Banaras as the city of the "Father of Modern Hindi," Bhartendu Harischandra, and the above-mentioned Premchand. The rich legacy of both of these writers is woven throughout these stories in their concern with the lives of the simple, downtrodden, and often forgotten side of India.

Rudra's acquaintances paint a picture of a powerful, no-nonsense man "who spoke his mind." At times he could be blunt and rough and at other times generous and easy-going, but perhaps the aspect of his personality which seems most striking is his angry torment. At the end of his life, the inner demons of anger seem to have demanded their due in the heavy consumption of *bhang* and alcohol. He died of TB in 1970, an enigmatic figure, generous supporter and contributor to Banaras' artistic life, yet known as a quarrelsome and angry man. He was respected for his creativity and learning, but also pitied because he did not make more use of his talents.

About this Translation

The language which Rudra uses in these stories might be described as a "composite" Hindi and does much to reflect the subject matter he has chosen to write about. On the one hand, he employs high literary Hindi; and on the other, he uses a very colorful, local dialect. The high literary quality comes from the frequent use of Sanskrit loan words. Sanskrit—the language of the Vedas and all other scripture of the Hindu tradition—along with Persian and Arabic is one of the main sources of vocabulary for modern Hindi. The relative "Sanskritization" of Rudra's Hindi reflects both the "Hindu-ness," as opposed to "Muslim-ness," of the writer (the son of a Hindu priest) and the subject material (mostly about Hindu life in a Hindu sacred place). The local color of the stories comes from the frequent use, especially in dialogue, of the Banarasi variant of *Bhoj Puri*. This dialect, of 40 million or more people living in the north Indian states of Uttar Pradesh and Bihar, is earthy—sometimes direct, and often loaded with sarcasm and double entendre—but also rich in poetry. As the language of the homes and streets of Banaras, *Bhoj Puri* is also the language of the most tender feelings and emotions of the city. Rudra draws heavily on the qualities of both his mother tongues in these stories, the one bringing to mind the sacred, immemorial quality of his city and the other, the organic, down-to-earth quality of everyday life.

Rudra's language, combining the high and low culture of his city, is like the other contrasts of these stories: secular and profane, priests and thugs, romance and sadness, classical literature and popular folk music. These contrasts reflect the unique character of this city where spiritual life, art, pleasure-seeking, and thuggery are constantly inter-mingling. It is my hope that some sense of this "composite" city of Ba-naras becomes available in the following pages.

Paul R. Golding
Washington, D.C.
October , 1994

1

Let's Sing the Praises
of the Revered Ganesh

Introduction

*Many in Banaras believe that the Maharajah of the city comes from
a lineage literally cursed by problems of succession. From the first Rajah
in 1738 until independence in 1948, seven Rajahs and Maharajahs have
ruled over Banaras. Yet, because of an absence of male heirs, all but
three of the rulers have been adopted from outside the family. This story,
set soon after 1738 when the current lineage of Banaras Rajahs and Maharajahs first assumed its place in the city, is one fictional account of
how that curse came about.*

*Caste, and especially the custom of marriage within one's own
caste, plays an important role in the tensions of this story. The two most
significant castes in mid-eighteenth century Banaras were the bhumihars
and the rajputs, also called thakurs. The first Rajah of Banaras was a
bhumihar while the adversaries in this story, the Thakur of Dhobhi and
his daughter, Panna, were rajputs. The Rajah's first marriage to a
woman of his caste produced only a daughter leaving no one to succeed
him. He then took a second wife of a different caste, violating social custom.*

*Some words and phrases in italic type are explained in a glossary at
the end of this story. Also, a postscript to this story, found after the glossary, contains notes on the fort at Gangapur, the ascendency of Raja
Balwant Singh in 18th century Banaras, and the use of references from
Indian epics.*

When *Goswami Tulsi Das* wrote, "Let's sing the praises of *Ganesh*" in his *Vinaya Patrika*, he could not even begin to imagine that this adoration of the Lord of Ganas would be the source of such marital strife and of a perpetual curse on the house of the founder of the current royal family of Banaras. He certainly could not have anticipated even one line from the following.

Rajah Balwant Singh was strolling along the wall of the Gangapur Fort with his friend and the commander of his army, Pandey Baijnath Singh, when he heard drumming and the clanging of metal *thalis*. This was followed by women singing the auspicious words, "Let's sing the praises of the revered Ganesh," and he realized that his wife, the queen or Rani Panna, had delivered a boy. He was spared the stigma of not having an heir to his throne. The singing ended suddenly in a tumultuous clamor of male voices. The rajah knew immediately that his relatives had interfered and had ordered the singing stopped. He had already received word that his cousin was wandering in the lanes of Kashi roaring like a bull, "Stop your drumming. Praise is not warranted on the birth of a bastard." Turning, the rajah said, "Did you hear this absurdity?"

"What absurdity, rajah?" Baijnath Singh asked sarcastically. "The father of the queen cut off your uncle's head and sent it to you. Your cousin is only taking his revenge. After all, it was his uncle also."

The rajah looked at Baijnath Singh with astonishment and said, "Revenge? That score was settled once and for all by your bravery. So, what kind of revenge is he taking out on my queen?"

"What do I know of these matters, your highness? Your cousin runs along the path you showed him," Baijnath said with such nonchalance as to elicit curiosity from the rajah.

"Surely you jest, Singh? What sort of raving nonsense is this?" The rajah pretended to be scolding.

"Me? Raving nonsense, Your Excellency?" Singh replied with a voice full of humility. "Remember? When your sword was broken in two pieces by the mace of the *Thakur* of Dhobhi, I ignored all the rules of *dharma* and interfered in your duel; and then, on your behalf, I killed him. Without their leader, the remaining soldiers fled, and you entered the fort without a man inside to stop you, Your Excellency."

Singh's words rang with pride. The rajah stayed silent, so his companion continued, "Your way was blocked by the daughter of that thakur, Panna, who stood in front of you with her hair unbraided, tears in her eyes, and a sickle in her hand."

The rajah said, "Don't you remember, Singh, that as soon as her eyes met mine, she dropped the sickle."

Baijnath Singh's head was shaking with intensity. "I remember, Your Excellency! You ordered her to be arrested. I stopped you, saying, 'Rajah, this is a woman, leave her.' What your cousin is doing, is taking his revenge by calling your new son a bastard and by making the other thakurs remember this incident, your excellency." Baijnath Singh folded his hands and stopped talking. He twisted his moustache with satisfaction at having made his point and looked at the rajah expectantly. Rather than respond, the rajah took a deep breath and bowed his head. Baijnath Singh smiled wanly and said softly, "To be frank, rajah, the only thing that grows on a tree of sin is sinful fruit."

"I know that, but what I didn't know is that even the son of a married woman would be called a 'bastard'."

"In the eyes of God, no. But in the eyes of society, yes."

The rajah responded with resignation. "Now I've come to my senses, Singh, and I realize that I've committed a great sin."

"So you should name the child for this. Name him *Chait* Singh. That's a name appropriate to one whose birth brought such an enlightenment."

3

"But what should I do about all the controversy that has been created by this birth?"

"Only time will resolve it, your highness."

"I will also try," the Rajah said as he headed off in the direction of the women's apartments, thinking about how to resolve this problem.

(2)

As soon as the boisterous men stopped the drum playing and thali banging, a blackness spread on the pale face of the Rani Panna, who was still suffering from the pain of delivery. With a mournful glance, she looked at the newborn infant lying with closed eyes on the maidservant's lap. A tearful smile broke out on her dry lips and then disappeared, like a feeble stream of water that vanishes on the desert soil. She got up and kissed the red-tinged forehead of the infant. In her heart, the river of motherly love overflowed. In her head, a storm of emotion raged, and like a cascade, tears burst out of her eyes.

The wise maidservant remained silent. She let the momentum of the storm take its course, and then, with sympathy, said, "What good will it do to bring so much suffering on yourself? After all, in the end, golden *Lanka* was burned along with everything else. You must endure."

With her large, full, black plum-like eyes looking at her trusted servant, Panna said, "How long should I burn in the fire of royalty, Lali? Sometimes my heart is filled with so much hate that I feel like plunging this dagger in the rajah's chest while he sleeps next to me, but..."

"What makes you stop?"

"The image that caused me to drop the sickle comes to me. So I put the dagger aside, and quietly lie down and shut my eyes. Then the image comes back and I can see it again," she said, closing her eyes as if to see something.

"Then you must be happy, Rani."

4

"How could I want more than the insult, disregard, and oppression that is being caused me, Lali! In my heart where this horrible hatred is being produced by these three offenses against me, could there be nothing of greater satisfaction!" An intensity had come into the Rani's voice.

Still panting from her effort, she said emotionally, "Just think how much enjoyment you would get by silently hating someone who is under the impression that because he pressures you and makes you helpless, you respect and venerate him."

With a poisonous, dull laugh, Panna tired and became quiet. Slowly she rolled her weary body back, flat on the bed. Lali, sensing the immense deadly hatred in the heart of the rani, turned pale. From her bed, Panna again said, "Today those people didn't allow the auspicious song to be sung on the birth of my first child. As soon as Ganeshji was installed, they came and turned the image to the wall. I can tell you this, Lali, that these people who are so proud of their lineage won't be able to rule for even three generations if they deprive me of my son's becoming a rajah at the cost of all the agony of my whole life. Every other generation to come will have to adopt a son in order to continue the lineage; and after three adoptions, their rule will end." The rani finished her statement with unblinking eyes, as if possessed by an evil spirit. And then seeing the rajah in front of her, she burst into loud sobs.

The rajah, pushing aside the curtain, stood on the threshold of the birth chamber. In a sorrowful and sympathetic tone, he said, "Don't make a curse, Rani. Your son will certainly rule after me. Set aside your anguish." The rajah glanced affectionately at the pale face of his rani. He had forgotten that the same ghee used to cool a burn also causes a fire to blaze. He was under the illusion that the rani had been weakened by his atrocities; that was why he had come to apply this ointment of sweet words. He didn't know that the rani was burning in the fire of disgrace; therefore, he was surprised when her expression suddenly turned dark, like a densely clouded sky. Her face became red, and sparks seemed to

5

come from her eyes. The rani was unable to stand the blow from the whip of his sympathy. She said angrily, "Don't sprinkle salt on the burn, rajah. If those people were able to disrupt the singing of the auspicious song on the birth of your son while you're still alive, do you think they'll allow him to become Rajah after his father has died? If you have any courage, have the veneration completed, rajah."

"My army backs me up because of my kinsmen, Rani. Because of political reasons...."

"Be quiet. Let me see how long your people will keep sacrificing the heart and pride of a woman for the sake of politics."

"Rani!" he said threateningly.

"I'm not scared, Rajah!" She went on haughtily, "I will not be scared. Your politics can stop the veneration on the birth of the prince from the womb of the rani, but neither you nor your relatives nor your politics can stop the mother from doing the veneration of her son on his day of birth. You understand this. Here, I will sing it. Call your relatives; let them try to stop me."

Doing as people do on the death of a family member, she started to pound her chest and sing as if crazed, "Let's sing the praises of the revered Ganesh, Let's sing the praises of the revered Ganesh."

GLOSSARY

Goswami Tulsi Das (ca 1543-1623). A poet who lived a part of his life in Banaras. He is most famous for his very popular version of the Hindu epic, the *Ramayana* (titled the *Ram Charit Manas*) and *Vinaya Pratrika.*

Ganesh. The corpulent, elephant-headed god who is the son of Lord Shiva and his consort, Parvati. Hindus believe that obtaining Ganesh's blessing at the beginning of an undertaking brings good fortune, and as "the remover of obstacles," his image may be seen above many a Banarasi threshold as a welcome to visitors.

Vinaya Patrika. A book, *A Little Letter of Humility*, by Goswami Tulsi Das written about 1600. This collection of devotional songs mostly to Ram from a humble devotee starts by introducing the reader to the gods, Ram's brothers, and others. The first god introduced is Ganesh, who is guarding the outer perimeter of the court where Ram sits.

Ganas. A group of semidivine spirits, or demigods, who are the attendant deities of Shiva. Ganesh is their Lord, and consequently is also referred to as Ganapati (i.e., Gana-Lord) or Ganeshvara.

Thali—a round metal plate.

Rani—wife of a rajah, a queen.

Kashi— "The City of Light," the most ancient of the many names for Banaras.

Thakur—literally, lord or master, but often used as an epithet for a person of the rajput or warrior caste.

Dharma—in its widest sense, this refers to the universal laws of nature that uphold the cosmos. Here it refers more narrowly to the code of conduct of the individual or group, and the belief that the practice of dharma leads to proper behavior and moral conduct.

Chait—Hindi word for enlightenment or awakening.

Lanka—the island kingdom of the demon king of the Ramayana, Ravan.

Ji. A suffix added to names to denote respect.

Ghee. Clarified butter.

POSTSCRIPT

The Fort at Gangapur

This story is set in the fort at Gangapur which stands these days in the village of that name about 10 miles west of Banaras. The Maharajah of Banaras holds a darbar, or royal assembly, at the fort a few days after the fall festival of Diwali and hosts a feast for the village's citizens. Half of the fort has been converted into "Balwant Singh Degree College" and the other half—a meeting and ceremonial garden—still stands, although in an increasingly dilapidated state. Nearby, a small shrine has been constructed where the villagers say Balwant Singh was born.

The Ascendency of Raja Balwant Singh
in 18th Century Banaras

These events occurred at a turbulent time in Banaras, and indeed, in Indian history. The decline of the Moghul empire, first noticeable in the early 1700s, had disrupted established loyalties and created a power vacuum which the British and other powers were jockeying to fill. The generalized tension of these times infuses this story.

For people in far away Banaras, the position of the Moghul emperor in Delhi had largely been replaced by the nawab, or regional ruler, of the state of Oudh based in Lucknow, about 250 miles northwest of Banaras. In the early 1700s, the nawab's officer in charge of Banaras was a Muslim, Mir Rustam Ali. He was a popular administrator, interested in his Hindu subjects' culture as can be seen today at Banaras Hindu University's art museum, where a painting of his participation in the Hindu festival of Holi is on display. The city's Mir Ghat bears his name.

POSTSCRIPT

The Fort at Gangapur

This story is set in the fort at Gangapur which stands these days in the village of that name about 10 miles west of Banaras. The Maharajah of Banaras holds a darbar, or royal assembly, at the fort a few days after the fall festival of Diwali and hosts a feast for the village's citizens. Half of the fort has been converted into "Balwant Singh Degree College" and the other half—a meeting and ceremonial garden—still stands, although in an increasingly dilapidated state. Nearby, a small shrine has been constructed where the villagers say Balwant Singh was born.

The Ascendency of Raja Balwant Singh
in 18th Century Banaras

These events occurred at a turbulent time in Banaras, and indeed, in Indian history. The decline of the Moghul empire, first noticeable in the early 1700s, had disrupted established loyalties and created a power vacuum which the British and other powers were jockeying to fill. The generalized tension of these times infuses this story.

For people in far away Banaras, the position of the Moghul emperor in Delhi had largely been replaced by the nawab, or regional ruler, of the state of Oudh based in Lucknow, about 250 miles northwest of Banaras. In the early 1700s, the nawab's officer in charge of Banaras was a Muslim, Mir Rustam Ali. He was a popular administrator, interested in his Hindu subjects' culture as can be seen today at Banaras Hindu University's art museum, where a painting of his participation in the Hindu festival of Holi is on display. The city's Mir Ghat bears his name.

9

As the governor of the Ghazipur, Jaunpur, and Banaras Districts, Mir Rustam Ali employed a Hindu named Mansa Ram to advise him and collect revenue in Banaras. Mansa Ram, the father of the first Rajah, sensing opportunities for his advancement, secured an army and fortified his home near Banaras in the village of Gangapur. Working around Mir Rustam Ali, in 1738, Mansa Ram managed to have the weakened Moghul emperor in Delhi appoint his son, Balwant Singh, Rajah of Banaras. As Rajah, Balwant Singh at first behaved like a subservient tax collector of the nawab, paying the tribute expected of him. But as soon as the nawab and emperor were distracted by invading Afghans, Balwant Singh stopped his payments and asserted the independence of his new Banaras Rajahdom.

The years that followed this rebellion were quite unsettled ones for the citizens of Banaras, since Balwant Singh's boldness and his success in taking control of the area from the hands of both emperor and nawab created a tempting target for other would-be Banaras rulers. During the years from 1748 to 1752, Balwant Singh had to contend with Afghans from the northwest, Marathas from the south and, finally, the nawab's forces in the north. After some close escapes, he came to terms again with the nawab in 1752 by agreeing to pay his tribute. However, he managed to retain de facto control over his Rajahdom. Balwant Singh then set out to consolidate his power in the region, first by constructing the great stone fort at Ramnagar, a mile south of Banaras, where his descendants still live today. He also took over several other forts in the area, expanding his Rajahdom by subjugating other local rajahs and lineages. Many of those subjugated were landowners and smaller rajahs like the Thakur of Dhobhi of this story.

Balwant Singh continued to rule until his death in 1770.[1] During the period of his reign, he succeeded in expanding his grip on the region and by the time of his death and succession by his son, Chait Singh, he had established himself as the paramount power in the area.

---

[1] Oldham, Wilton, *Historical and Statistical Memoir of the Ghazeepoor District*, Government Press, North-Western Provinces, Allahabad, 1870.

Figure 2. The view north from what today is known as Chait Singh Palace from Captain Robert Elliot's Views of the East, published in 1833. It was from this place that the Rajah Chait Singh is said to have fled British troops.

2

A Saddle on the Elephant and
a Howdah on the Horse

Introduction

A popular Banaras story relates how, in 1781, the second Rajah of Banaras escaped arrest by the troops of the British Governor General, Warren Hastings. Hastings had come to collect more taxes from the Rajah to finance British expansion in India. Instead, the Governor General was lucky to flee the city with his life. Although occurring two centuries ago, this act of defiance by Rajah Chait Singh—the background for this short story—is still a point of pride with the city's citizens.

The title comes from a type of song called a "bin"—a limerick. This limerick is in the style of the poet Kabir (1440-1518), who often wrote of reversals or contradictions such as that described here where a howdah, a platform placed on the back of an elephant containing seats for riders, is placed on a horse and the saddle intended for the horse is placed on the back of an elephant.

Some words and phrases in italic type are explained in a glossary at the end of this story. Also, a postscript to this story, found after the glossary, contains notes on Chait Singh's escape, the Banaras Rajah in the nineteenth and twentieth centuries, names in India, and the nine-planets ceremony.

Hello *Guru*. I touch your feet! Lotan Baheliay said, folding his hands, and looking at Nagar Guru coming from the direction of the Kabir intersection.

"May your spirit remain blissful!" Nagar answered. After giving this blessing, he saw behind Lotan the strange sight of a horse carrying a howdah on its back and an elephant with a saddle. About two dozen of the Rajah's soldiers had surrounded the two animals. He asked Lotan, "What's going on here?"

"What do you think? This is by order of the Queen Mother. You didn't hear? Warren Hastings and the company of British soldiers fled."

Nagar was curious. He took hold of Lotan's hand and pulled him to the stoop where today the building of Jayanmandal-Yatraliya is located. A stillness had spread over the city. For the last two days, all kinds of rumors were flying. Yesterday, in order to collect a fine, Warren Hastings himself had come to Kashi from Calcutta. The Rajah and his subjects were all scared. The Rajah's army had become listless and indolent. The residents of the city were spiritless.

After sitting down on the stoop, Lotan very quietly told Nagar that even though everyone was frightened, the Queen Mother, Panna, had managed to keep her wits about her. She had all the shopkeepers of the city summoned for the fight that would take place in the lanes of the city. She got them to agree that they would hide twenty to thirty soldiers in each of their houses. When Warren Hastings got word of what was going on, he didn't even wait for the sun to come up before he fled to *Chunar*. Pointing in front of him, Lotan said, "Once Warren Hastings realized what was going on, he went to hide over there in that fodder storage room. When I told this to the king's mother, she said, 'Now we have an opportunity to put some spirit into the citizenry of Banaras. Put a saddle on an elephant and a howdah on a horse, so

13

"Listen to the children shout, and look, here comes Labadan Sahua. Where could he be taking his family? That bastard had the message delivered to me that he wasn't home. Well, if he wasn't home, where's he coming from now?" Lotan jumped from the stoop, and Nagar followed him.

Meanwhile, Sahua's slim second wife, fair complexioned, but unsteady like a mare without reins, and holding a box of jewelry ever more tightly under her arm, said to the shouting children who had formed a procession around the horse and elephant, "You worms, behave yourselves!"

Then the senior wife thundered at the children, "May you be struck by lightening!" Big and heavy like an elephant, she carried a bundle of thick blankets and clothes on her head. A thick layer of red powder was pasted on her forehead and in the part of her hair.

Sudin, the sickly twenty-year-old son of the senior wife, and Goura, the nine-year-old daughter of the junior wife, repeated what their mothers said, like echoes coming from different ends of the horizon. Meanwhile, that ball of tobacco, the husband, Labadan, was saying, "Wait, you sons of bitches," to the group of children who kept on shouting . Fleeing quickly, after putting a howdah on a horse and a saddle on an elephant, Sahua and his family could not understand more of the chant than this. He thought that the children were making fun of him, that they were calling one of his wives an elephant and the other one a horse, and that by the howdah they meant the large box of jewelry and by the saddle they meant the blankets. Sahua believed that the children were saying he and his family were the ones who were fleeing.

After leaving his house, he indeed was fleeing. Considering the slogan to be entirely directed at him, he became angry. Suddenly Sahua used his walking stick to hit a little boy. The boy, seeing the stick about to come down on his hand, ran away, but still got a little splinter. After this Sahua had to sit down on the

14

stoop and catch his breath. The boy started to laugh. On top of all the tension of the day, Sahua broke out crying like a bull.

Suddenly, a sharp slap fell on his cheek. Two teeth fell on the street in front of him. A small flow of blood trickled out of his mouth. He raised his eyes and saw that Nagar Guru was standing in front of him asking, "Why did you hit the boy? Speak up!"

"Ask the bastard why he was running away," Lotan Baheliay said.

Labadan was in the midst of a great crisis. Could it be that because it was his birthday, the day was turning out to be so inauspicious? Right from the morning, a quarrel had started, the consequences of which were still unfolding this evening. His son, afflicted with the "European disease," had a mouth full of blisters.* * Sahua did not know exactly what the "European disease" meant, but he considered it a shameful ailment and was wondering what would happen with this affliction. So when he opened his eyes this morning and saw the wilted face of his son, his heart turned bitter. He glared angrily at his son. The young man, however, thought that his father's expression was meant to convey some sympathy. Collecting all the pain in his heart that he could manage, the son said with a voice choked in anticipation of receiving sympathy, "Father, it hurts so much I can't spit."

The father, whose voice had dissolved in the overheated molten lead of his hate-filled and angry heart, replied, "So if you can't spit, don't worry. The whole world would like to spit at you."

The son, hearing this, frowned and went away. But his mother, who had been standing nearby grinding spices, created a *Mahabharata* over this remark. She started a shower of piercing comments to the effect that Sahua had lost his heart. He got angry at her and said, "You black-faced bitch, you buffalo. So early in the morning, the roots of my ears are crackling."

---

* See glossary

15

The senior wife answered in a similar vein, "You worthless dog, you bastard, so early in the morning you start to curse my son. If someone should be unfortunate enough to say your name early in the morning, he won't see food all day."

What she said to a certain extent was true. Because of Sahua's miserliness, people really did not mention his name in the morning—so, the senior wife's words were like a dagger piercing his heart. If it hadn't been his birthday, he would never have let her comment pass without answering back. But today, he needed the peaceful cooperation of his wives to complete the nine-planets ceremony. So, to prevent his senior wife's further outrage and whatever would follow from it, he swallowed the insult as if it were a bitter drink, and started to console his senior wife. The junior wife, coming to his aid in an effort to promote her standing with him, emptily reassured her cowife, "Let it go. After all, he said it to his own son, not to some stranger."

Finally, the senior wife calmed down, and the atmosphere in the house became a little more tolerable. Because all activity in the city had come to a standstill for the last two days, the materials needed for the ceremonies of the nine-planet worship and fire sacrifice could not easily be found. Borrowing and begging from his neighbors, Sahua managed to assemble what he needed; but the *Pundit* refused to come to carry out the ceremony. Instead he responded, "The situation in the city is dangerous. The king is locked in his own palace. The army of the invading foreigners is patrolling the streets. I'm not such a fool that I'd go out under these circumstances. And if I were to put my life in danger, I wouldn't do it for one-and-a-half *paisas'* worth of food."

When Sahua received this message, he was at his wit's end. He was proud of his own straight-forwardness—saying rough, insensitive, and stupid things, but he despaired when he heard the Pundit's no-nonsense refusal. For her own part, the junior wife, hoping that her status might increase by taking part in the ceremony, realized that her own lucky sun might be setting with

16

the Pundit's refusal. At first she felt helpless. But then, clinging like fire to the tobacco-stained body of Sahua, she said suggestively, "If you are not with us, what good would all your wealth be to us. Have another Pundit summoned."

So another Pundit came to perform the ceremony. This one was promised five paisas' worth of rice. After tying his clothing to that of his wives, Sahua carefully read the *mantra;* and offering water in place of money, the nine-planet worship was completed. Then the fire sacrifice got underway. Because Sahua didn't provide enough *ghee,* the fire's flame wouldn't blaze up. Goura, the junior wife's daughter, was fanning the fire to coax some flames out of it when suddenly some sparks fell on her hands and face. Sympathy came from everyone, but Sahua laughed and said cheerfully, "Dear daughter, if you lost your courage with just a couple of sparks, what will you do when its time for your *suttee*?"

The Pundit, stunned by this insensitivity, stared at Sahua. Goura, who hadn't understood anything, started to laugh; but her mother was outraged. Unable to fight openly in front of a stranger, she made a clucking sound, untied the knot between the piece of cloth she was wearing over her sari and Sahua's shawl, and stood up, still very upset. At this point, even Sahua realized his mistake, but the arrow had already been shot. He helplessly took in the expression of his junior wife. The senior wife caught her cowife's hand and pulled her close, "Let it go. After all, he said it to his own daughter, not to some stranger." Then she re-tied the knot.

The junior wife looked angrily out of the corner of her eye, but said no more. The fire sacrifice ended without further incident. But the distress that had befallen Sahua had yet to run its course. He was sitting down to eat when Lotan Baheliay shouted from the lane below, "Is Sahua there, is Labadan in?"

Labadan Sahua peeked out of a small window. He saw the bodyguard of the Maharajah Chait Singh wearing a green coat, with a turban made of cloth folds of gold embroidery, twisted here and there and studded with gold, and with a sword fastened to a

17

pink cummerbund around his waist. Lotan was shouting, holding an axe in one hand. Sahua whispered to Goura, "Tell him that father isn't home!" She stuck her head out of the window and repeated the message.

"When he comes back, tell him to come to the palace. This is by order of the queen mother," Baheliay said and went on his way. When he overheard the queen mother's message, Sahua's heart filled with dread. He supposed that the summons was to squeeze money out of him. He started to worry.

Labadan's early years in business had been spent going around the lanes of Kashi shouting, "Four *ramdan laddus* for one paisa." Scraping together a paisa here and there, he opened his first sweet shop in the Nikas market. As his stomach expanded, his value in the market went up, and his health deteriorated. Now a rich merchant, he was concerned with the king's designs on the wealth he had accumulated. The junior wife consoled him and suggested a solution, "Nothing good will come from worrying. The money is hidden safely away in the ground. Let's pack some clothes and bedding and go and hide somewhere else. We can go to my parents' and wait for the problem to blow over there."

Sahua liked the idea. They packed up some things and started off in the direction of his in-laws in Karan-Ganta. But then, on the way, this ugly incident happened. Sahua feared for his life. He heard Baheliay's words, looked at Nagar tearfully, and threw himself at his feet.

Nagar felt sorry for him but asked harshly, "So tell us, why did you hit the boy?"

Sahua, still lying stretched out straight as a stick on the ground at Nagar's feet, answered, "It was not my fault, Guru. The children were making fun of our running away."

"They were making fun of you?" Nagar asked, surprised. He couldn't understand how this matter of Warren Hastings' escape was making fun of Sahua. Sahua, hiding his shame about his wives being considered a horse and an elephant, would only say,

18

"You were also listening, Guru. Didn't you hear what the children were saying?"

"What were they saying? Repeat it," Nagar said.

Looking around him, ashamed, Sahua only said, "The children said this:

Fleeing quickly, after putting a Howdah on a horse and a saddle on an elephant, Labadan Sudin fled."

Both Nagar and Lotan broke out laughing. Nagar said, "Damn it, Sahua wasn't able to understand that the slogan referred to Warren Hastings and not to him." Nagar gave Sahua a kick and went on. The crowd of children chanted their slogan:

"Fleeing quickly, after putting a howdah on a horse and a saddle on an elephant, Warren Hastings fled."

Sahua made a face and said, "Oh, no."

GLOSSARY

Guru—a teacher or spiritual guide, and in Banaras also used as a term of respect.

Chunar—a fort about 25 miles downstream from Banaras.

European disease—probably syphilis.

Mahabharata—one of the great epics of Indian literature about a family's bitter rivalry that results in a great intrafamily war. In this story, the epic's title is invoked to symbolize family tensions and fighting.

Pundit—a name of respect applied to learned people. Often, as in this story, the pundit is a Brahmin and a priest.

Paisa—the smallest monetary unit of the rupee, one hundred of which equal one rupee.

Mantra—verbal formulas or prayers, usually in Sanskrit, carrying a deep meaning and/or magical potency.

Ghee—clarified butter, which in this story is placed in the fire to make it flare.

Suttee—the (now illegal) Hindu rite of suicide of widows by self-immolation on their husband's funeral pyre.

Ramdan laddu—a special, round sweet made of ramdan, a wheat grain, which is usually the cheapest grain available in the market. The sweet and grain are often considered edible during festivals when fasting rules do not permit eating other grains.

POSTSCRIPT

Chait Singh's Escape from the British

In their effort to assert authority over North India, the British made an agreement in 1775 with the Nawab of Oudh (in Lucknow) that gave them control over Banaras. At first preoccupied elsewhere in their expanding territory, the British chose to exercise control indirectly, allowing the Rajah, Chait Singh, to collect taxes and pass on a share to the East India Company. This arrangement worked for a while, but by 1781 a dispute arose over the amount due the "Company," which by that time was in need of more cash to wage war against the French in Madras and elsewhere.[1] The background to this story is the British effort to collect these funds.

The British Governor General, Warren Hastings, added a hefty fine to the amount of back taxes due, and set out from Calcutta to pressure the Rajah to pay up. When he arrived in Banaras, Hastings had the Rajah placed under house arrest at Shivala Ghat in what today is known as Chait Singh Palace. In response to Hastings' action, the Rajah's supporters attacked the under-armed British and their Indian soldiers. Taking advantage of the confusion, Chait Singh tied together the long cloths of several turbans, hung them out the back of his house, and slid down this makeshift rope to the river's edge, escaping to the other side. Soon thereafter, Hastings heard rumors of an impending mass uprising against his presence and fled the city to a garrison at Chunar, about 30 miles upstream of Banaras. The place in Banaras where Warren Hastings stayed is today marked by a metal plaque near the Kabir intersection, the scene at the opening of this story.

This resistance to British expansion was linked to a series of power struggles that were taking place throughout north India at the time. The Mogul empire's influence had all but disappeared, and the British were on the verge of expanding their territory from Calcutta and Bihar, westward. The Nawab of Oudh, hoping to gain some time to consolidate his power, aligned himself with the British. Against him were his mother

---

[1] Oldham, Wilton, *Historical and Statistical Memoir of the Ghazeepoor District*, Government Press, North-Western Provinces, Allahabad, 1870, pp 106-17.

and grandmother who supported Chait Singh. The result was this revolt in Banaras and throughout most of the region around Banaras against the British presence in the area.

Although the incident in the story portrays Chait Singh victorious against a British presence, the victory was short-lived. Working with the Nawab, Hastings managed to bring the regional situation back under British control within a few months. In Banaras itself, Hastings returned with more troops a month after he fled and regained the city. At that time, he named a grandson of Balwant Singh (through a wife other than Chait Singh's mother, the Panna of the previous story) to be Rajah. Chait Singh spent the remaining 30 years of his life in exile in central India.[1]

The Banaras Rajah in the Nineteenth and Twentieth Centuries

The subsequent history of the Banaras Rajahdom is one of first losing and then regaining power, depending primarily upon what suited British colonial purposes. At the close of the eighteenth century and through most of the nineteenth century, the British administered the Banaras region directly. During this time, the Rajah was officially only a large landowner, although he had important political and cultural influence in the region. By the late nineteenth century, as a reward for remaining loyal to the British in the 1857 uprising, the Rajah was given the more prestigious title of Maharajah. In the early twentieth century, the British created a new princely state out of the Maharajah's land as a counterweight to emerging nationalist concerns. They did not, however, include Banaras in this state; and instead, the British maintained direct control over the city. At independence, this princely state was abolished.[2]

---

[1] Barnett, Richard B., *North India Between Empires*, Berkeley, University of California Press, 1980, and Marshall, Peter J., *The Impeachment of Warren Hastings*, London, Oxford University Press, 1965.

[2] Freitag, Sandria B., "Introduction: The History and Political Economy of Banaras," in *Culture and Power in Banaras*, ed. Sandria Freitag, University of California Press, 1989, pp. 10-1.

In India names often convey one's caste, place of origin, and status. For example, the first name mentioned in the story, Lotan Baheliay, tells a Banarasi reader that he is from a low caste whose traditional work is bird catching. This Baheliay has found other employment, but even today, members of the Baheliay caste may be found selling their prey as pets or, for a fee, they will set pairs of male and female birds free as a kind of donation to gain religious merit. A market of such birds caught by people of the Baheliay caste is held daily at dusk in front of the main telegraph office in Banaras in Niche Bhag, near Chauk.

Baheliays' lower status, relative to that of the second character in the story, Nagar, is conveyed by his greeting (i.e., touching Nagar's feet, or at least saying that he does so) and by his adding the title "guru" to Nagar's name. Nagar's name indicates that he is a Brahmin, and that his family, like many in Banaras, migrated from the west Indian state of Gujarat.

The name of the third character, Labadan Sahua, tells us that he is from a caste of merchants. His status as a wealthy merchant is defined by the fact that he has two wives. Polygamy, an old practice among Hindus, is a sign of wealth often associated with kings and chiefs.

Names may also bring bad luck. According to a common north Indian folk belief, to say or hear certain unlucky names in the morning will bring bad luck for the rest of the day, as will seeing an unlucky face right after awaking in the morning. In the story both beliefs play a role when Sahua insults his diseased son for being in his sight upon Sahua's waking and when Sahua's senior wife scolds him that to say his name in the morning will surely bring bad luck.

The Nine-planets Ceremony

During this story, a household ceremony is performed for the main character's birthday—an auspicious occasion that the gods may bless by granting a boon or curse with catastrophe. For this reason, the character has chosen to honor the nine planets of the solar system—gods, especially Saturn, who have the potential to create great misfortune and can be quite difficult for humans to connect with. As part of the ceremony, the main participant offers coins to the planets. These are

23

intended as tokens of respect to the various gods of the planets and are usually retained by the priest. Here, the participant offers only water, a sign of his parsimony. After this the Brahmin priest, referred to as "Pundit", carries out a ceremony in which several substances are offered, by way of a sacrifice, to the god of fire. When the ceremony is over, the Brahmin priest is often remunerated with uncooked food, since by the strict rules of purity observed by Brahmins, he does not wish to eat food cooked outside his own house.

Figure 3. A view of the main ghat of Banaras, Dashashvamedha, from
Louis Rousselet, *L'Inde des Rajahs*, published in 1875.

3

Nagar's Boat is Leaving for Kalapani, Oh Hari!

Introduction

The word gunda *in modern Hindi means hoodlum or rogue. To be called a* gunda *today is definitely not a compliment. However, once upon a time in Banaras' history—the period of this story—to be called a* gunda *was something to be proud of. In those days, a* gunda *was a kind of warrior, out to correct the evils of society—an Indian Robin Hood. Every Banarasi knows about the most famous of the old-time* gundas, *such as Dataram Nagar of this story or Bhangar Bhikshuk of the following story. The residents of Banaras recite their adventures and frequently use them as examples of bravery, courage, and temperance.*

The title of this story is taken from a type of folk song called a kajli. Kajlis are usually sung in the rainy season, at night, in competitions between groups or individuals representing different neighborhoods or wrestling clubs. The word "Hari" at the end of this title refers to Vishnu and his avatar or incarnation Krishna.

Some words and phrases in italic type *are explained in a glossary at the end of this story. Also, a postscript to this story, found after the glossary, contains notes on* gundas *in eighteenth-century Banaras and folk beliefs about owls, iron, and the number 16.*

26

The judge delivered the sentence to Talvarya Dataram Nagar: 20 years in prison on Kalapani Island. His friends—already cleared on similar charges—broke out crying inconsolably. Even the stonelike hearts of these brave men were moved. Bound with handcuffs and shackles, Nagar's strong body tensed straight like a rod, heedless of the iron constraints placed upon him. The red veins of his eyes brightened even more. A hate-filled smile spread on his lips, and he cast an admonishing glance at the judge. Their eyes met; but the judge, unable to bear the fire of his gaze, looked down. He mumbled under his breath, "A brave man!" But Nagar, not hearing him, shifted his attention to his friends and followers. Throwing an angry glance at them, he thundered, "Why are you crying like impotent men? Twenty years isn't even a day in the life of *Brahma*. It'll pass with the snap of a finger. Now, tell *Babaji* that he has the responsibility for my household. And tell the *Mirzapur* Baba ji that he should look after Sundar. Go! Get along."

After receiving their leader's orders, Nagar's followers left the courtroom with heavy hearts and wet eyes. Nagar stood on his tiptoes and stretched. As he twisted his body to the right and left, his flexed biceps shook like swimming fish, and his joints cracked. The shackles clanged, and swaying like a bound lion, he left the room with the guards following.

2

The *Kashi* of 1772 was famous for its gundas. After *Warren Hastings* looted Kashi, the new foreign rulers forced these warriors to sheath their swords, and left them with little alternative but to become gundas in order to earn their livelihoods. They had seen what happened under Chait Singh when Kashi had lost its spirit, and they knew that the sons of Chait Singh were little more than hooligans and unworthy to lead. So, with no alternative but to follow the rule of the jungle, the gang leaders took a vow of hatred against the foreigners.

The most important of these gang leaders were Dataram Nagar and Bhangar Bhikshuk. In Alaipur, next to where today the hospital for contagious diseases stands, in the garden of the Tirth of Ei-trani-baitrani, is Bhikshuk's well. You won't find that garden today, but the well is still there where Nagar's *akhara* was located. In the akhara, Nagar's followers used to gather and plan their attacks on the foreigners and their Indian accomplices. Of the latter, the most important in Banaras were Shambhu Ram Pandit, Beni Ram Pandit, Molvi Alaudin, and Kubara and Munshi Faiz Ali, and in Mirzapur, the contractor Banakat Misir. Kubara had already been killed by Babu Nanaku Singh Najib during the escape of Rajah Chait Singh. Beni Ram and Shambhu Ram were scared and seldom came out of their houses. Because he was the British-appointed Deputy Administrator of Banaras, Munshi Faiz Ali was well protected; and because he lived in Mirzapur, Banakat Misir considered himself out of danger. Nonetheless, in the opinion of Nagar's friends, the score was to be settled first of all with Misir in Mirzapur. So, Nagar sent his brothers, Shyamu and Bitthal, to deliver the message to Misir that he was inviting him for *bhang* by the *Ojhala stream* during the next full moon. Misir accepted and by return message said he'd supply the food.

(3)

Lying in the small cramped jail cell, Nagar was taking account of his life. He was sure that Umaravgiri, the son of the brave and courageous Rajah of Jhansi, would see that no harm came to his family living in Kashi; and that in Mirzapur, Gosai Jayaram Giri would see that Sundar received what she needed to survive.

The thought of Sundar made him recall the incident of *Ojhala stream* where Misir showed up with a hundred fighters from *Akori*

28

Virohi—Nagar, accompanied by a platoon of his brothers, friends, and followers, had already arrived before Misir. On one side of the site, bhang was being ground on twenty-five mill stones, and on the other side, *puris* were being fried in large pans.

After consuming all the bhang and food in the moonlit night, the two camps started their bloody fight. In the middle of it, Misir shouted, "Hail to the *goddess Vindyavasini!*" At the same time, Nagar challenged with a, "Hail to *Hatakeshvar,* " and the battle was on. The two leaders moved away from their respective gangs and began their own fight, one on one. Nagar attacked with his sword, and Misir used his *lathi* to deflect the charge. But then the lathi broke into pieces. Misir moved back, while Nagar kept up the assault. Then Misir turned and fled. Nagar chased him. In the moonlight, Nagar would not lose sight of Misir. Suddenly, it occurred to Nagar that running after an enemy was sinful. He stopped.

The shackles of the fettered Nagar clanged as the thought of that glorious chapter of his life made his chest swell. The mosquitos in the small cell had their fill of his blood. Their attack was over. The chained-up Nagar was able to close his eyes. But his waking thoughts kept hovering in his brain and became the dreams of sleep.

He was returning after he stopped chasing Misir. It was midnight. The full 16 portions of the moonlight were shining. On the other side of the stream, an owl sitting on a babul tree hooted over and over. The moonlight shone off the white wings of a heron, which was putting all the weight of its body on one leg, hoping to surprise a fish. Under Nagar's feet, the yellow earth, warmed from the day, had become tender and cold in the smooth light. The stillness of the quiet night, the intense moonlight, the distant sleeping forest—all filled the atmosphere with pathos. Taking all of this in, he suddenly noticed a white, bundle-like object lying close to a hillock in front of him. He kept his glance fixed on the object and became aware of a woman hiding there under a cloth.

29

The hairs on Nagar's body tingled. He was trembling, and his heart was pounding. As he stared blankly around him, his hand fell to his sword. The shine of the sword ascended to his eyes, and then he recalled that ghosts cannot stay put in the reflection of iron. He raised the sword and went forward. As he approached, a woman's form arose. She looked at Nagar—embarrassed, frightened, and hesitant. Nagar returned her look with his eyes opened wide, as if to ask what she was.

She became assured, seeing the manful figure of Nagar. His thin, black moustache was pointed upward. On one side of his waist was a knife, and on the other side he had tucked a dagger. His muscular, well-built, and exercised body, his wavy curly hair, and the red threads in his eyes took her hesitancy away. She laughed boldly and grasped his hand.

As if electricity had run through Nagar's body, his muscles tightened. He looked at her longingly, with lust. His hand went forward and pulled the beautiful woman toward him. She seemed to him to be like a fine wine that he must have. The young woman resisted as Nagar came to his senses, letting go of her. She almost fell.

Nagar had suddenly recalled his father's words at the time Nagar took his vow of courage: "Those who take this vow must look on all women as their mothers." It was his father who established the Nagar Brahmin's family deity, Hatakeshvar, in Kashi. Getting hold of himself, he asked her sharply, "Who are you?"

"Is this the proper way to ask such a question?" the woman retorted.

Nagar took two steps back. His heart, which had never hardened before a woman, had now regained its natural tenderness. Resigned, he asked, "All right, but do me the kindness of telling me who you are."

The woman laughed, and then answered, "Previously, I was the unmarried, virgin daughter of a prestigious *thakur*, and now I am someone's concubine."

30

"How did this happen?" Nagar asked.

"In the same way as you, when you came just now, acted like any man, and then became like a god."

"Who made you a concubine?"

"Everything is the work of Misir *Maharaj*. A year ago, I was picking mangos in my orchard when Misir had me abducted and treated me worse than a concubine."

"What brought you here now?"

"I heard that someone was going to settle a score with Misir. So, I came to see that Misir's head would be cut off and that my heart's angry fire would be quenched."

"Now what are you going to do?"

"What can I say? As Misir was fleeing, he saw me here. I'm sure I'll meet a cruel end. Now you are my refuge."

Nagar thought a few minutes and said, "Go to Nar Ghat. I'll meet you there later."

Lying on the hard ground, the prisoner shifted to his other side. A sweet smile ran across his torture-stiffened face. The dream caught hold of the prisoner.

Nagar left the young woman and started off again. On the trail in front of him was a path so narrow that only one person at a time could pass. Nagar saw Misir walking there. But Misir, hearing Nagar's shouts, wouldn't even turn around. He kept moving further away.

"Wait up, Maharaj!" Nagar shouted.

"Come forward, Nagar!" Misir answered without turning. Nagar, surprised by the boldness in Misir's voice, said, "Misirji, you are without weapons and I am armed. What if I should attack you from behind?"

Misir laughed loudly, and said, "I know you're a gunda, and can't do such an underhanded thing."

Nagar, immersed in simple pride, answered, "So then why did you run away on the open field?"

31

"You saw my broken lathi, and yet still you were aggressive. You had forgotten that you should not assault an unarmed enemy."

"But Misir ji, it is you who has behaved immorally. You have sold your country into the hands of foreigners. And then you disgraced a virgin princess. For these crimes, you must fight with me."

"But I'm still empty-handed, brother."

"That doesn't matter. I'll drop my sword. You may take my knife or my dagger, whichever you want, and then let's settle this."

Lines came and went on his face as the thrust and counter-thrust of the fight ensued in his dream. As he sighed on the battle-field after his dagger pierced Misir's heart, so also Nagar took a long, deep breath when this happened in his dream.

He opened his eyes. The dream had made him worry. He had generously given refuge to the outcast Sundar, arranging for her to live in a rented house on Nar Ghat. To make her more self-sufficient, he hired professionals from Mirzapur to teach her music and singing. Whenever he went to Mirzapur, he saw that all her needs were taken care of, and then before nightfall, he would always leave, never spending the night there.

Nagar called her "Sundar," and she seemed to him as beautiful as the name.

(4)

The moon of the dark fortnight of *Shravan* had risen in the sky. The prisoner took a cold breath. His chains were pinching and hurting him. He considered his present situation, and started to think about the circumstances that had brought him to this point.

While in Mirzapur, he received the news that the Deputy Administrator, Faiz Ali, again was trying to lead the horse of the *Muharrami* procession through Thatheri Bazaar in Banaras. For the last two years, since the establishment of the East India Company,

32

Faiz Ali had been trying to take a new route for the procession, and twice Nagar had prevented its passing. This time, however, Nagar heard that Faiz Ali had arranged for a platoon of soldiers as an escort. Nagar's blood boiled up. He returned straight from Mirzapur, going by way of Sunriya to Thatheri bazaar. Just as he arrived, he saw the horse passing in front of him. He brandished his sword and cut the animal in two. The horse collapsed, and the platoon fell on Nagar. Nagar's sword stood against the bayonets of the white soldiers and the swords of the natives. The bayonets were broken, as Nagar's sword advanced, cutting a swath through the remaining obstacles.

Nagar hid himself inside a stream-fed well in the Brahmanal area. One night, realizing that he wasn't safe there, he moved to hide in a cave at Raj Ghat. A few days later, when he was going for fresh air, informers spotted him.

When the British received this news, they dispatched an army of native soldiers to surround him. With nothing but a metal water pot, he managed to break the skulls of a few soldiers, but then he was arrested.

After reviewing the story of his life, Nagar felt that it had meaning. He was satisfied.

(5)

It was the ninth night of the dark fortnight of Shravan—two days after word of Nagar's sentencing had been received. The moon rose in a clouded sky. In the dull light, one could see only the outlines of objects, their exact shapes remaining blurred. Here and there the clouds broke, and in one corner of the sky a star was twinkling. At that time, Gosai Jayaram Giri, Bhangar Bhikshuk, and another follower of Nagar, Biraju, descended from their horse-drawn carriage in the village of Chilh and boarded a boat to cross the river to Nar Ghat. They didn't know that Sundar had already received the news of Nagar's Kalapani sentence. They also didn't know that just then on the other side of the river, Sundar

33

was sitting on the steps of Nar Ghat, looking up at the sky, and swinging her feet distractedly in the water of the great Ganges. She was wondering:

What, really, is this blue sky over our heads? Beyond this sky, is there some place like this earth filled with happiness, sadness, laughter, and tears; where there are colorful vines, fruits, and flowers? Are there men and women like we have here? Are there also unhappy, homeless people? Is there our kind of prejudice and insensitivity? My acquaintance with Nagar was so short; but still, he behaved as if we had known one another for many former lives. But that Nagar went off to Kalapani.

Sundar started to think, "Where is Kalapani? It's far, very far, an island from which no one returns." Sundar's heart filled, her lips quivered. She started to sing:

"Nagar's boat is going to Kalapani, oh Hari!
Everybody else's boat is going to Kashi Vishvanath,
oh Rama,
But Nagar's boat is going to Kalapani, oh Hari!"

Her voice gradually became louder. Her moving chant echoed in the sky, piercing the silence. The deserted, rocky shore, the rippling waves, and the companions of Nagar, riding in their boat, heard:

"At home, weep Nagar's mother and sister, oh Rama,
On the bed, weeps the young wife, oh Hari!
On the wall pegs, weep Nagar's shield and sword, oh Rama!
In the corner, Nagar's rifle is crying, oh Hari!"

The boat had come closer. The three passengers heard: On their way, weep your friends and companions, oh Rama, On Nar Ghat, weeps a concubine, oh Hari!

The three started to sob. The boatman rowed more quickly, and the boat came right in front of Sundar. But Sundar kept singing, completely engrossed in her own thoughts:

If I had known that you would go to Kalapani, oh Rama, I would have come to you as a bride, oh Hari!"

34

Above the wind was crying, below the waves of the Ganges were moaning; and in the boat, the tear-filled eyes of the boatman and his three passengers were competing with a river swollen by spring rains.

For a long time afterwards, the residents of Mirzapur gave money to the insane woman of Nar Ghat—purchasing the touching sorrow of her song. The eyes of the listeners would fill when she would dissolve all the pain of her heart and sing-

Nagar's boat is going to Kalapani, oh Hari!

GLOSSARY

Kalapani—the Nicobar and Andaman Islands in the Bay of Bengal, where the British authorities used to send prisoners.

Brahma—the god usually associated with the creation of the universe. A day in Brahma's life is said to be equal to over 4 billion years by human reckoning.

Babaji—term of respect used for an older person.

Mirzapur—a small city on the shores of the Ganges, about 50 miles upstream from Banaras. Mirzapur was a major port and trading center along the river when the Ganges was an important route of commerce, before the construction of the railroad. Because it offered many opportunities for piracy, the city used to have an unsavory reputation as a hideout for thieves and murderers and a center of prostitution and dancing women. Even today, the Mirzapur *lathi,* a stick associated with gang warfare, is one of the city's best-known products.

Kashi—"City of Light," the most ancient of the many names for Banaras.

Warren Hastings—the British Governor-General.

Akhara—a kind of meeting place or club where men practice martial arts and physically exercise.

Bhang—an intoxicating drink made from hemp.

Ojhala stream and Akori Virohi—two place names associated with a famous pilgrimage center near Mirzapur named Vindyahachal.

Puris—a type of deep-fried bread.

Goddess Vindyavasini—the goddess of the main temple at the famous pilgrimage center of Vindyahachal near Mirzapur.

Hatakeshvar—a form of Shiva meaning literally the "golden Shiva." According to the story this was established in Banaras by Nagar's family.

Lathi—A stick about three or four feet long used for fighting.

Thakur—literally, lord or master, but often used as an epithet for a person of the rajput or warrior caste.

Maharaj—a term of respect and authority.

Sundar—a Hindi word and name meaning beautiful.

Shravan—a month in the Hindu calendar that falls in July-
August.

Muharram—a Muslim festival commemorating the death of the mar-
tyred grandson of Mohammed, Imam Husain. During the festival, a
procession led by a horse winds over the northern part of Banaras.
The horse stands for Husain's faithful animal who delivered the news
of his master's death to his followers.

Thatheri Bazaar—an important, predominately Hindu, market noted for
metal goods.

Kashi Vishvanath—the main Shiva temple in Banaras.

Rama—an avatar or incarnation of the god Visnu who appeared on earth
as the king of Ayodhya. His story forms the central part of the epic,
the *Ramayana.*

POSTSCRIPT

Gundas in Eighteenth-Century Banaras

Gundas are perhaps best described in the following quote from a story of the famous Banaras writer and poet of a half-century ago, Jai Shankar Prasad. In his short story, *"Gunda,"* he describes the wretched state of eighteenth-century Banaras. In those days, even the learned religious ascetics had no place in the violence-prone city, where their monasteries and temples had been destroyed. He writes about a new cult that grew up in response to this state of affairs, a cult of *"gundas."*

The cult's religion was bravery. To die on one's word, to seize one's livelihood with courage, to avoid using weapons on wounded enemies and on cowards who beg for mercy, to render help to the suppressed poor of the society, and to live each moment as if it might be their last was the cult's creed. The citizens of Kashi called this cult, "Gunda".[1]

Because a factual historical record of the gundas does not exist, the legends about them seem to come out of the rich folklore of Banaras, possibly reflecting considerable idealization. In reality, they may have been little more than chiefs of various warlord groups in the neighborhoods of Banaras. But in these stories, they have become romanticized for their opposition to the British, their courage in righting the insults to Hinduism, and their chivalrous respect for women. Seen retrospectively after the Indian independence movement and compared to modern hooliganism and corruption, the gundas of old may indeed look appealing today.

Folk Beliefs about Owls, Iron, and the Number Sixteen

Just as the popularity of Banaras' gundas comes out of the city's thriving folk tradition, so the author has filled this story with other folk beliefs still common in Banaras. An example is the fear inspired by the hoot of an owl. Contrary to their image in the West as wise birds, owls

---

[1] This quote was taken from the short story, "Gunda" published in a collection of Hindi short stories by Jai Shanker Prasad, *Indrajaal*, New Delhi, Bhartiya Grant Niketan, 1988, p. 65.

are considered stupid and inauspicious animals in north India. Hence, an owl's hoot indicates that something is amiss, that a ghost may appear or some other frightening incident take place. Another such belief from the story is iron's ability to repel ghosts. Often, for example, grooms wear a little sword of iron during their wedding ceremony, or midwives place iron in the birthing room to make sure that a ghost does not appear at critical moments. A last such belief is the notion that the whole of something is made up of 16 parts. In this story the full moon is described as being of 16 portions.

Figure 4.—A view southward of Aurangzeb Mosque and Panchaganga Ghat from Captain Robert Elliot's *Views of the East*, published in 1833. The prominent spot now occupied by the mosque once was the site of the Bindu Madharav Temple mentioned in the following story.

41

4

My Beloved's Bed is on a Spike

Introduction

The main character of this story, Bhangar Bhikshuk, is a gunda like the character in the previous story. However, this gunda is engaged not only in outward struggles with the British and their agents, he is also grappling with his soul. He is a Hindu, an asceti, and a warrior, who has renounced his marriage and is torn by the question of whether he should reverse his vow of renunciation.

"Warrior ascetics" like Bhangar Bhikshuk were not uncommon in the chaotic circumstances of eighteenth-century north India. In fact, militancy in the name of religion seems to go back at least to the arrival of Islam in the twelfth century, and then was strongly stimulated by the withering of central (Moghul) authority in the late 1700s.[1] The tradition continues today, as evidenced by the several sects involved in current conflicts such as the struggle on the part of militant Hindus to remove a mosque allegedly built in 1528 on the site of a temple at Ram's birthplace in Ayodhya, north India.

The title of this story and a number of references later are associated with the Hindu poet and mystic devotee of Lord Krishna, Mira Bai, believed to have lived about 1500. In her passionate songs to Lord Krishna, she often referred to him as her beloved. The song associated with the title, like many of her songs, captures her longing to be reunited with her beloved. This, however, is unattainable; the marriage bed is described as being located above a suli, *or a type of spike, used as an ancient form of capital punishment on which a victim was impaled.*

---

[1] Lorenzen, David N., "Warrior Ascetics in Indian History," *Journal of the American Oriental Society,* Vol. 98, No. 1, 1978, pp. 61-74

Some words and phrases in italics are explained in a glossary at the end of this story. Also, a postscript to this story, found after the glossary, contains notes on renunciation in Hinduism, Shaivite, and Vaishnava sectarianism, parallels between the two main characters in the story and the lives of Mira Bai and Kalidasa, and drug taking for ritual purposes in India.

(1)

Dhuga-dhug, dhuga-dhug, dhuga-dhug! At the eastern gate of *Chandni Chauk,* the crier beat his drum, and shouted, "The world belongs to God, the ruler of the country is the *Badshah,* and these orders come from the East India Company... Anyone who can provide information leading to the arrest of Bhangar Bhikshuk will be given five hundred silver rupees as a reward, and whoever knowingly hides information about him will suffer for the crime—dhuga-dhug, dhuga-dhug, dhuga-dhug!"

And then on the other side, by the northern gate, the jingling of cymbals and another drumming sound came—"dhab, dhab, dhabadhab, dhab, dhabadhab, dhab." Beating his drum with gusto, Bhangar Bhikshuk himself entered the bazaar. In his melodious, pain-filled, high-pitched voice he was singing the *lavni:*

"To know one's pain, don't ask Vishnu,
Brahma, Buddha, or those wandering Sadhus,
Better is to ask the throat of the blue-throated Shiva
to know the pleasure of drinking poison."

Attracted by the sweet tinkling of his voice, as if it were the strings of a *veena,* people came out of their stores and homes. The crier also recognized that voice and, hiding his drum in a thick, double-fold bag, went away.

The residents of Kashi were both amazed by and infatuated with the colorful personality and daring of Bhikshuk. As always, he had tied an ochre-colored lungi around his waist and, even though it was cold, he was wearing no other piece of clothing

43

except a gold-brocaded shawl.[*] Oiled, curly, beetle black hair was waving on his shoulders; and just under his ears, on the side of his white, shaven face, were two wide, curving, long sideburns. The combination of the wavy hair, sideburns, and his white face made it look as though a snake with 1000 tails and two hands was holding tightly to a box of gold—his face.

His smiling lips were colored red with the juice of *pan,* and on his large rolling eyes, dazed by *bhang,* there was a thick line of *surma.* On each ear was a *rudraksha bead,* and a crystal necklace hung around his neck. The three horizontal lines of a *tripand,* made from ash, glistened on his forehead; and in the middle of the tripand was a vermillion-colored *tikka.* A frightening, thick-bladed axe was hanging over one shoulder. Behind him a crowd of hundreds had formed.

The perfume sellers running after him were anointing him with perfume, the garland sellers were dressing his hair with garlands, and the rich merchants and money lenders were giving him money. For these people, he embodied the heroic side of Kashi. To Banarasis, he and Dataram Nagar were considered equal to the pair of Ram and Lakshman; months ago, Dataram Nagar was sent to Kalapani, and from that very day Bhikshuk had disappeared from the city. Today, people came running from wherever they were, all over the city, to see Bhikshuk. On Shivala Ghat, the English graves were testimony to Bhikshuk's manliness; and today, in connection with this incident, the drums were being beaten for his arrest.

After strolling around the square, singing and playing his instruments for an hour or so, Bhikshuk climbed on the high platform of the Shiva temple in the middle of the bazaar, and proclaimed, "Respected people, you have all heard the drum beating and its message. Five hundred silver rupees is no small sum. Whoever is eager to claim this reward, come forward."

---

[*] See glossary

44

Some among those present laughed, some stayed silent, and the remainder started to look with frightened eyes toward the courthouse. Right above the southern entrance of Chandni Chauk—which today is called Gundri Bazaar—was the courthouse of those days. Nobody near Bhikshuk came forward, and no one even peeked out of the courthouse. When he saw this, Bhikshuk smiled in a way which on the face of woman might make her look unchaste and lustful—but on his face the smile made him look godly. Casting this smile on the crowd, he said, "Good, now I'll get along to the police inspector and see how eager he is."

(2)

Evening was approaching; it was the month of *Paush*. The beat of the *tabla* could be heard in the upper story of Amirjan *Tavayaf's* splendid mansion in *Dal Mandi*. The flames of the candles hanging in the glass holders on the wall had already started to shine. Garlands of flowers were hung over the awnings of the windows. With the help of the cymbals, a *sarangi,* and the drum beat, Amirjan was practicing her *raga,* "Oh, *Papiha bird,* do not sing your song—it will remind me of my lover."

Amirjan was coming to the end of the first stanza when she heard some commotion from the lane outside. She saw a group of prostitutes near her looking out of the window to see what was happening. Approaching, she saw Bhangar Bhikshuk moving along slowly and dreamily in the lane, tossing money to cripples, beggars, and the old. Behind him was a large crowd. The famous, beautiful dancing women of the city were all standing at their windows, but Bhangar Bhikshuk, busy looking around him, did not have a chance to look up. Amirjan, the most famous of the city's dancing women, could not tolerate this affront to her beauty. She was accustomed to everyone singing her praises. A mere note of music from her voice gave her the power of a demon, and a melody turned her into Satan. On the strength of her

45

music and beauty, she ruled men's hearts and in the end, after extracting all that was in them, tossed them aside.

Like others, she looked at Bhikshuk and became infatuated with his appearance. But more than others, in beholding Bhikshuk, she was saddened that the pearl of her precious smile, instead of falling into his eyes, fell in the dust of the street. To get his attention, she suddenly took off her fine woolen yellow shawl and threw it on Bhikshuk.

A startled Bhikshuk, pulling the shawl off, looked up. Their eyes met. A knife-sharp smile filled with the pride of victory played on the lips of Amirjan, but it didn't last long. Bhikshuk took aim and swung his money bag, landing it with a cracking sound on the tip of Amirjan's nose. Blood started to drip as if a Lakshman had again cut off the nose of a *Shurpanakha.* Bhikshuk burst out laughing.

At that very moment, a pitiful, ugly, old beggar woman came out of a nearby mosque. She was wearing patched pajamas, a torn *kurta*, and, over these, in the name of a shawl, was a tattered rag. She had seen the exchange between Bhikshuk and the dancing woman. A strange sound came out of her wrinkled toothless face—it could have been a laugh or a cough. She stopped, leaned on her walking stick, and then straightened up, touched Bhikshuk's chin with her dirty fingers and said, "Well done! For that, my son, you have all my respect!"

The crowd standing nearby was apprehensive that an angry Bhikshuk might push the old lady. But instead—as they could tell by his voice and by his look—he was full of curiosity. He asked, "What are you doing here? Well, since you have come, you must not go without taking something." So saying, he put Amirjan's fine shawl on the old lady's decrepit, shivering body, and moved on before the old lady could express even a sentence of gratitude.

And so he arrived at the police station. The number of people following Bhikshuk had by now come to over a thousand. Everyone was curious to see what would happen. Even the children of the city knew about the strength and courage of Bhikshuk, about his erudition and his weaponry, his expertise in wrestling, and his devotion to music. Similarly, in a short time, the people of Kashi had already had a taste of the heartless restrictions of the law and order of the new English rulers. The people were certain that today, something fantastic, "unique, and worth seeing" would surely happen. By nature a people who loved spectacle, the citizens of Kashi had their longing awakened by Bhikshuk's actions. However, by the time they had arrived at the police station, the cowards in the crowd and those who'd just come along for the spectacle had sneaked away, leaving only his serious supporters.

In front of the present police station at Chauk, where today the *tongas* and buggies await passengers, there used to be a well, and all around the well was a field. In the Kashi of those days, a solitary stand was set up every night to sell *gol-guppe-kachalu*. The police headquarters used to be on the footpath of the road, just in front of the southern side of the present-day police station. Bhikshuk got up on the high wall of the well, and facing the police building, shouted, "Hey, Mr. Chief of Police, Bhikshuk has come up to your doorstep. What are you going to do about it?"

The chief of police didn't have the courage to utter a word, and the few guards who were standing at the gate ran inside. Bhikshuk let out a peal of laughter like a thunderbolt from the terrifying *Bhairav*. The curiosity of the assembled crowd had cooled. People realized that Bhikshuk had got the best of the authorities. They weren't surprised because they knew that, as in the past, the authorities accepted defeat from people like Bhikshuk, and that they would continue to do so in the future. With the crowd's veneration for him increased, Bhikshuk crossed through the Kucha Ajayab Singh (present-day Kachauri Gali) with several companions and went to his retreat at *Panchaganga Ghat.*

47

3

Bhikshuk's body was exhausted, and his mind was worn out with worry. He had been on the move continuously since yesterday morning. Not only hadn't he slept, but he hadn't had the opportunity even to sit. So, he rested on a stone pedestal on the ghat by the shore of the Ganges. He reclined facing east, across the river. Meanwhile, his friends had started to make plans to enjoy themselves with bhang and other intoxicants.

It was a winter evening. The full, snow-white moon of the month of Paush had set out on its nightly journey. On the other side of the river, a rising mist was slowly trying to envelop everything in sight, making it look like a beautiful, moon-faced woman who, sitting on the shore of the *heavenly Ganges*, had hung her dense hair over the earthly Ganges. From there, nothing of the far shore was visible, but Bhikshuk wanted only to see the other side.

He wanted to see the white, two-storey mud house hidden under that black sheet of mist. He wanted to see Mangala *Gauri,* the beautiful, fair mistress living in that white house. Yesterday, Mangala Gauri saved his life by a hair's breadth. As soon as she saw him, she recognized him. But Bhikshuk only recognized her when she, with her long and slender eyes filled with tears and her voice overwhelmed by sadness, asked, "Has the ascetic penance of Gauri not yet been completed?" And then after he recognized her, he promised that on the next night he would come to her. From that moment, he had been struggling with a question: can something renounced be taken back?

Mangala Gauri was his wife. But he had only seen her twice in his life—once on the evening of their wedding, and then thirteen years later, last night.

Bhikshuk was born into a family of the *Charan* caste. But his family, instead of carrying on their traditional occupation of wandering minstrels, were more engaged in war and battle. So, from his birth, Bhikshuk was exposed more to the art of waging war than to that of reading poetry and singing. When he was thirteen years old, his wedding was held in Jaisalmer.

His father-in-law was a famous Charan minstrel of Rajasthan. Kings had often rewarded him handsomely. In his later years, he took an oath of initiation at the *"Nath-Dvar"* temple of Udaipur.

Right after this, the first child of his house was born—a girl. She was the apple of her father's eye. Naturally, the father's religious ways rubbed off on the girl. While the father was saying his prayers, the daughter, still lisping in youth, would dance and sing, "I will dance in front of Krishna."

Bhikshuk recalled the incident of his wedding night. After he had made the seven rounds about the sacred fire, the women of his in-law's house requested him to recite poetry.* In response, he just kept silent. The reason: Until then he hadn't even been accustomed to pronouncing his name properly. Instead of saying Chandrachur, he could only say Chanarchur. The women's response to his silence echoed like the twinging noise of a bow in his ears: "He's a fool!"

The magic of the artful *Brahma* was present there as well. Exhausted from staying awake all night, young, newly wed Mangala, who had memorized hundreds of such couplets and poems, echoed, "Yes, he's a fool!"

He was illiterate, but not stupid. And if by chance an uneducated person happens to be strong and powerful, there is no limit to what his ego will allow. He got up and, pushing aside the group of women, went outside. He ran into the wild darkness, hiding himself in the night. For months, he crossed the desert until he arrived at Kashi. There he studied, became a scholar, and never returned to his village.

Bhikshuk's stream of thoughts ended. A friend approached him and said, *"Guru,* it's ready."

---

* See glossary

"It's very cold. Today I'll mix myself a drink with the *five intoxicants*," Bhikshuk said.

"Fine, it'll be ready in a few minutes," his companion answered.

Bhikshuk placed two strips of arsenic on the grinding board together with the datura seeds and nagbach and started to grind them together with his share of bhang. When it was ready, he put a little opium in the middle, and with a little water swallowed the whole thing straight down to his stomach. He stood up and made the sky echo with his tune, and the waves of the Ganges repeated it: To know the pleasure of drinking poison, ask the throat of Shiva.

(4)

At 10 o'clock in the evening, after Bhikshuk had taken eleven straight dips in the Ganges, he felt as if his intoxication lost its edge under the assault of the cold. His friends had left, and having dried himself, he went into his cave by the side of the ghat. A light was burning in a clay lamp, and a tiger skin was spread on the floor. He sat down on the tiger skin, and puffing away on some *ganja,* he started to think. Until now he had not analyzed the question of whether it was proper to take something back that he had renounced. Both sides of the question appeared before him— "What's renounced is impure. Listen, don't take her back. A woman will be an obstacle to your devotion to God. After all, you are a religious devotee."

But in the next moment, he would think, "Gauri is my wife. She's as beautiful as she is intelligent. She will help me in carrying out my duties. I took her hand in marriage, and her protection is my responsibility, as her husband. I made her a promise and she must be waiting for me." In considering this question, his recollection of the responsibilities of a Hindu husband decided the matter. Overwhelmed, he slowly came out of the cave. He untied a boat, and while he sat down to row into the river, his mind flowed in its own stream of thoughts. Working the oars automatically, he was thinking: "If she had not come, surely the authorities would have caught me. I was tired, empty-handed, and on foot. They were armed and on horseback. I don't know how those scoundrels recognized me. They chased me from Ali Nagar to Kateysar. But they must have realized they'd met their match. I managed to leave all of them behind, except that damned constable. He was chasing behind me until the end."

The boat reached the shore. Bhikshuk stood on the land. He fastened the boat to a stake in the sand, and went off alone toward the village. Jackals, their faces raised to the pale moon, were howling. Just as he arrived in the village, dogs started following him, barking. When he reached the front of Mangala Gauri's compound, he saw that very constable sitting on a wooden stool, stroking his moustache, and loudly singing a few stanzas from the *Ramayana*:

"O birds and deer, O string of bees,
Have you seen the fawn-eyed Sita?
You have nothing to fear; you may enjoy yourselves at will,
progeny of deer.
He has come in search of a gold deer."

Bhikshuk was standing right behind the trough where he had hidden himself the previous night. At that time, he was thirsty, and in an attempt to drink, he tripped over a stake used for tying oxen. Gauri was standing there giving fodder to the oxen. She came towards him and, when she saw him, was shaken. Nearing him, she heard the sound of horses' hooves and pointed to the trough, saying with an emotion-choked voice, "Hide there, under the trough."

And so, he managed to hide from danger as the constable rode up, asking, "Gauri, has anyone come running by here just now?" Without hesitating for even a moment, Gauri answered, "No, I've been by the door for the last two hours."

51

Hearing this the constable said, "Oh well, at least you might be able to give me some water."

As he was recalling this incident of the previous evening, Bhikshuk saw the door open in front of him, and Gauri came out carrying a bowl of milk. She asked the constable something. He smiled, took the bowl from her, and put it to his mouth. Bhikshuk felt as if a whip had landed on his back. He ran quickly to the Ganges, untied the boat, and sat down. As he rowed, he started cursing himself:

Oh, even though I'm educated, I'm still a fool! I dressed my lust in the garb of sex. In a momentary attraction, I was going to destroy the devotion of my entire lifetime. I didn't even wonder once how this Gauri had come here from Jaisalmer. And now she is living with this man whom she talks to after he smiles at her, and to whom she feeds a bowl of milk.

Bhikshuk's hands were churning the water with the oars, just as his mind was churning the uneasy ideas in his head. With the freshness of a heavy wind, his mind was calming down and the stream of thoughts were turning away from his self-criticism. His lips started to move with his strong emotions, and the thoughts came out, mumbled.

This is what happens when you decide something without understanding all the implications. On the basis of nothing more than guesses, things worry me that I do not know much about. Perhaps the constable is just some close relative of hers. What was wrong in his asking for something after meeting her? But the fact is, in spite of all the devotion I've achieved, I'm just like everyone else. Like on my wedding night, the *internal enemies* have awakened in me again. Otherwise, having heard about the price on my head, why would I go around all day in the city challenging the authorities as I did? There was a huge crowd with me; and because of this, no one had the courage to confront me. If not for that crowd, I know very well what would have happened to me if caught. Nagar went to Kalapani. I would be hanged.

Because of my jealousy, I was going to commit an injustice to Gauri for the second time.

And then, even after crossing more than half the Ganges, he turned the boat around and headed back again in the direction of the Katesar bridge. Just as he was turning the boat, he was shocked to see British soldiers approaching him in 20 boats coming from the direction of the fort. He turned his boat quickly back toward Banaras and saw the soldiers aiming their guns in his direction. Before they could fire a shot, he jumped in the water. Staying submerged as much as possible, he reached the shore and staggered into his cave with the speed of an arrow, like a lion trapped in the middle of a hunt. The soldiers also disembarked from their boats and stood in front of his door.

(5)

A joyous sound, raised up by hundreds of lips, rolled over the waves of the Ganges, ran up the sand of the shore, flew over the green, crop-filled fields, entered the two-storey house of the Constable Yadunath, and after clashing against the eardrums of Mangala Gauri, woke her up. Pursuing the sound, she peeked outside the hole in the southern wall. Through an opening in the dark trees, she saw that dark field, the sand-filled shore, and then across the Ganges, a dark, black, snake-like coil of smoke pouring from the turret atop the *Bindu Madharav* Temple.

Last night, Gauri didn't sleep. Even though she was accustomed to sleeping on the ground, she had prepared a bed on which she placed an embroidered sheet. But, the one who was to sleep in that bed never came. Without desiring it, when the southern wind started to blow in the dawn, she fell asleep after waiting awake the whole night. And now upon awakening, she was seeing that it wasn't only in her eye and in her mind that a fire was raging, but also on the other side of the river. Suddenly, someone knocked on the door. Gauri opened it, and Genda, the energetic, good-natured daughter of a neighbor, entered the room like a storm. Hanging herself like a garland around Gauri's neck, she said, "Big sister, I've been calling you for so long! Screaming so much has made my throat sore. What were you doing?"

"Genda, what's so important that you want me this early in the morning?" Gauri said with a smile while releasing her neck from Genda's hold. The carefree, 13-year-old Genda had nothing special in mind for Gauri to do. She only came to tell her that there was a fire on the other side of the river. So she said, "Everyone in the village has gone to take a look at a fire on the other side. I also went up to the shore."

"Oh, I see!" Gauri said pretending to be surprised.

"What do you mean—you see? I thought that I should come and get you to take a look. I shouted for so long standing under your window! Usually you get up with the dawn at four and sing who knows what songs. Today, I didn't even hear your voice. Sing that song, "Oh, Krishna accept me as your slave." After she said this, Genda burst out laughing, and then becoming serious, she said, "Really, where did you learn all those songs?"

The carefree Genda was asking question after question, without realizing that each question was like a hammer blow to Gauri's head. Gauri said, "There's not much to it. My father was a devotee of Krishna, and I learned everything from him. After he died, his sons-in-law took all my property, and I came to my uncle's. Then, when my uncle got a job in the Banaras Rajah's army, I came here with him."

"Good, now sing just one song, sister dear! I like it very much," Genda said.

"I'm not really in the mood, Genda. Some other time."

"No, no, please, my sweet sister, just sing two or three stanzas," Genda kept insisting like a child. Finally, Gauri bowed to her stubbornness. Looking at the empty bed, she started to hum:

"Oh, I have lost my mind over this pain,

54

Nobody knows my pain.
The bed of my beloved is right on top of the spike,
How will there ever be a meeting?"

"Who is the one you want to meet, sister dear? You don't mean the one that was hiding under the trough the night before last?" Genda asked, laughing loudly.

"Oh, you naughty girl, stop it!" Gauri said and she heard her uncle calling her from the first floor, "Gauri, Gauri! You still haven't come down. What's going on?"

She heard the sound of her uncle coming up the stairs. So that he wouldn't come into the room and see the bed, she went outside with Genda and, meeting him there, nonchalantly asked, "What is it, uncle?"

"It's our bad luck, daughter! That unfortunate person met a dog's death today. If I had arrested him the day before yesterday, I'd have five hundred silver rupees in my hand now." Hearing this, Gauri lost all feeling. But keeping her face blank, she quickly got hold of herself, and not even an "Oh" came out of her mouth. Genda asked Yadunath, "Who was it that died a dog's death, Uncle?"

"Oh, it was the companion of that gang leader Nagar, Bhangar Bhikshuk. But listen, daughter, he was really brave. Those six or seven British soldiers who stuck their heads in his cave never lived to withdraw them. In the end, the army covered the front of the cave with wood and set fire to it. Look over there. What a flame!"

Both Gauri and Genda started to look at the fiery destruction to the west. Gauri saw the wavering flames springing up in an effort to touch the sky, as if they were the red bloodied fingers of some soul, reaching upward. The line of smoke had taken the shape of a metal spike, and on the tip of this spike sat Bhangar Bhikshuk, gradually ascending. She thought a moment and said to Genda, "Go downstairs. I'll be right down after I close up the room."

55

Genda descended. Gauri went back into the room. She closed the door from inside. In the corner, a dim lamp was flickering. She picked it up and set flame to the bed sheet spread over the bed. In an instant the flame caught. She set the same lamp's flame to the end of her sari and for the first time in 12 years stepped on the bed. In an instant Genda and Yadunath realized that there was a fire in Gauri's room. Genda ran upstairs and knocking on the door shouted, "Sister, sister, what's going on?"

Like the fearsome, victorious laugh that *Kali* issued while killing the demons, Gauri's voice came from inside: "Genda, my beloved's bed is on the end of the spike, this is how I will meet him!" After this came the disagreeable smell of burning flesh and wood.

GLOSSARY
(in order of appearance in the text)

Chandni Chauk—literally the "moonlight square," the name for the old city center in many north Indian cities.

Badshah—the Moghul emperor.

Lavni—a kind of folk song.

Veena—a stringed musical instrument, considered the most subtle and sacred of Hindu instruments.

Kashi—"The city of Light," the most ancient of the many names for Banaras.

Ochre-colored Lungi—a piece of cloth wrapped around the waist like a skirt, the color of which indicates that the wearer is a brahmachari, a celibate.

Pan—a mixture of betel nut, lime, and other ingredients wrapped in a betel leaf. When chewed, it mixes with saliva into a bright red color.

Bhang—an intoxicating food made from hemp.

Surma—(collyrium) a medicinal powder made from the ash of pearls and other substances.

Rudraksha bead—the peach pit-like seed worn by followers of Shiva. The beads are said to be the tears of Shiva emitted by his third eye when he contemplates the destruction of the world.

Tripand—Three horizontal lines of moist ash worn on the forehead of a follower of Shiva.

Tikka dot—a dot of color, in this case vermillion, daubed ritually in the middle of the forehead.

Ram and Lakshman—the two brotherly heroes of the Hindu epic, the *Ramayana.*

Paush—a month of the Hindu calendar occuring during February and March.

Tabla—a pair of drums.

Tavayaf—a title (sometimes as a last name) signifying that the bearer is a dancing woman and prostitute.

Dal Mandi—the main Muslim bazaar in the center of Banaras.

Sarangi—a nonfretted musical instrument.

Raga—a class of nodal melodies which constitute the basis of an Indian music composition.

Papiha bird—a type of Cuckoo bird often mentioned in Hindi literature to symbolize the idea of lovelorn beings.

Shurpanakha—the sister of the evil king of Lanka (Ravana) who proposed marriage to Ram in the *Ramayana*. In response to her proposal, the brother of Ram, Lakshman, cut off her nose.

Kurta—a type of collarless shirt extending as far as the knees, with an open button neck.

Tonga—a horse-drawn carriage.

Gol-guppe-kachalu—a popular Banaras street snack consisting of a piece of dough filled with a fried potato mixture and coated with a green, coriander sauce.

Bhairav—a deity, born out of the blood of Shiva, who has a frightening and awe-inspiring aspect.

Panchaganga Ghat—One of the main bathing ghats in Banaras consisting of stairs leading down to the river.

Heavenly Ganges—one of three Ganges—heavenly (i.e., the milky way), earthly (i.e., that which flows through Banaras), and one in the nether world.

Gauri—A name for Shiva's consort, Parvati, associated with one of the popular stories of how Shiva and Parvati were married. According to this version of events, Parvati took to asceticism to win Shiva's love. The white heat of her terrible penances made her glow with a fair-skinned divine beauty. From this image came the name Gauri, which means bright or golden one, for Parvati. Eventually, impressed by her penance, Shiva accepted Parvati as his wife.

Charan—A Rajastani caste whose traditional occupation was composing and singing poetry extolling their patron's virtues and accomplishments, as well as those of the patron's ancestors. In addition to performing at court, they also have performed at weddings and feasts.

Nath-Dvar—(the door of God)an important pilgrimage site in Rajastan for devotees of Krishna.

Seven rounds about the sacred fire—In the final part of a Hindu wedding ceremony, the bride and groom together circumambulate a sacred fire. The marriage is complete and irrevocable with the taking of the seventh turn.

Brahma—the creator and also the god who decides what course one's life will follow, who will marry whom, what sort of a match it will be, etc.

Guru—a teacher or spiritual guide, and in Banaras also widely used as a term of respect.

Five intoxicants—arsenic, datura seed (atropine), nagbach (aconite), bhang, and opium.

Ganja—an intoxicant, like bhang, from the hemp plant.

Six internal enemies—worldly desire, ego, anger, greed, worldly attachment, and pride.

Bindu Madharav (Drop of Krishna) Temple—an important Krishna/Vishnu temple located on Panchaganga Ghat near the Aurangzeb Mosque. Nearby is the principal Banaras temple to the goddess, Mangala Gauri.

Kali—The fearsome warrior goddess noted for her world-saving ability to drink the blood of demons who otherwise would be able to re-create themselves from spilled blood.

POSTSCRIPT

Renunciation

The struggle of the main character over his renunciation is rooted in Hindu philosophy, where to renounce something that one desires brings one closer to the ideal of release or liberation. To use the terminology of Hinduism, one's soul, or *atman,* once freed from the illusion, or *maya,* of its individuality as manifested through desire, *kama,* becomes identified completely with the Absolute. This awareness of the identification of *atman* with the Absolute or *Brahman* puts one on the path to the ultimate religious goal of *moksha,* which is liberation from the eternal cycle of rebirth.

From the story, we are able to know that Bhikshuk has renounced relations with women, but as a gunda, he combines this with a life of action, and if need be, violence. Consequently he must grapple with the issue of whether his action is carried out in a way consistent with the dictates of his spiritual development. That is, in performing any action, he must not be concerned with or attracted to the results of his action, for that would imply he has not yet quenched his desires, his attachments to this world. As the god Krishna says in the *Bhagavad Gita,* "On action alone be thy interest, never its fruits."

Shaivite and Vaishnava Sectarianism

Another feature of the character, Bhangar Bhikshuk, is that he is a shaivite, a devotee of the god Shiva. This is conveyed at the beginning when he sings the song about the blue-throated Shiva, a reference to the mythological event when Lord Shiva swallowed poison to save the world from destruction. To prevent his own destruction, Shiva kept the poison in his throat, the cause of its blue color. Bhikshuk's shaivism is also conveyed by his wearing a *rudraksha* bead, the peach pit-like seed used to make a kind of rosary and said to be the tears emitted by Shiva's third eye when he contemplates the destruction of the world. Furthermore, Bhikshuk has the Shaivite's *tripand,* or three-colored horizontal lines, glistening on his forehead, and he takes bhang, Shiva's favorite intoxicant. Another characteristic shared with Shiva is that Bhangar

60

Bhikshuk's wife is named Mangala Gauri, which is one of the names for Parvati, Shiva's consort.

The sectarian differences between Shaivites and the followers of Vishnu—called generally Vaishnavas—concern theological and ritual distinctions and interest only a small part of the Indian population. While one sect directs its devotion primarily to Vishnu, his avatars, and their consorts, the other worships Shiva and the gods and goddesses associated with him. A few social generalizations can be made about their differences—such as that Vaishnavas tend to be more observant of caste and dietary restrictions, while Shaivites allow for more esoteric and unconventional worship and behavior. Within each group, however, there are many exceptions.

Parallels to Mira Bai

Many of the verses sung by Mangla Gauri in this story are attributed to Mira Bai, a Hindu poet and mystic who lived in the sixteenth century in Rajasthan. Legend has it that at an early age, after her husband's death, she surrendered her life to the worship of Krishna, and incurred the displeasure of her late husband's family for not behaving as a traditional widow. Her life in some respects parallels Gauri's in this story.

Parallels to Kalidasa

The account of Bhangar Bhikshuk's wedding parallels the legend of Kalidas, a great Sanskrit dramatist who is believed to have lived sometime between A.D. 350-600. Very little is known authoritatively about his life; however, one of the legends attributed to him in his youth is that he was very handsome, but dull and uneducated. Through the trickery of some ministers, a princess was convinced to accept him in marriage. When she discovered his ignorance and coarseness, she insulted him. Kalidas ran away to Banaras and, years later, became a great scholar.

Drug Taking for Ritual Purposes

Taking drugs for ritual purposes has a long tradition in Hinduism dating at least to the days of the vedic sacrifices (ca 1200 B.C.) when the

61

juice of the *soma* plant figured prominently in ritual. In Puranic (i.e., from ca 200 B.C. to A.D. 800) Indian mythology, this practice is strongly linked with the god Shiva who is especially fond of *bhang,* one of the five intoxicants mentioned above. Also, the mixture of drugs and poisons appears to be a very old practice in Banaras. To save the world from destruction, Lord Shiva once had to swallow such a potent combination of poisons that he had to leave them in his neck in order to survive. To be able to withstand the effects of these combinations is viewed as a type of *siddhi* or penance. Even today in Banaras, on certain occasions, poisons are said to be taken mixed with intoxicants.

Figure 5.—The interior of a Harem as sketched by Wm. Daniell in his *tableaux Pittoresques de L'Inde*, published in 1835.

5

Coming to Me, Coming to Me

Introduction

This story opens in early nineteenth-century Banaras in the midst of Hindu-Muslim riots. The story takes place in a part of the city called Jnana Vapi—the "well of wisdom," a place rich with the symbols of conflict between the adherents of these two religions even today. On one side of Jnana Vapi is the Vishvanath Temple--the most important temple in Banaras because it houses a Shiva lingam (the ithyphallic representation of Shiva) that is said to have been placed there by Lord Shiva himself. On another side of Jnana Vapi is the Alamgiri Mosque, an important place of worship for Muslims today.

In the background of this story is another type of conflict having to do with how men and women see one another and the demand by women in India for more freedom. This struggle also has a long history which seems to be even more intense in India today.

The story's title is from part of a line of a Tumari, a type of devotional folksong which usually expresses the love of the milkmaid, Radha, for Lord Krishna.

Some words and phrases in italic type are explained in a glossary at the end of the story. Also, a postscript to this story, found after the glossary, contains notes on the history of this period and on the position of women in India.

64

(1)

On that day, the muezzin of the Alamgiri Mosque in Jnana Vapi did not climb up to the minaret to chant the namaz and wake up the faithful from their deep sleep. The worshipers, who every morning go to the recently rebuilt Vishvanath temple after taking their bath in the Ganges, did not make the lane under the temple echo with "Har, Har, Mahadev Shambho." The watchman, who every morning opens the area's gate and shouts, "It's four o'clock, wake up!" did not make his last round. But the caged-in parrot hanging on the veranda of the two-story house in front of the mosque, did call out his customary, "Radha Shyam, Radha Shyam!"

Just below the cage, on an old, worn mattress stretched out on a broken-down cot, the old, almost blind painter, Ram Dayal, heard his parrot's cries, and opened his eyes. He *yawned*, lifted his hand in front of his mouth, and snapped his fingers a few times.[*] "Radha Shyam, Radha Shyam," he echoed.

He yawned again, opened his mouth and rested his hand in front of it, saying, "If Amiran doesn't come again today, then....?" And the series of yawns continued.

For the last three days, there had been no trace of old Amiran, the seller of opium-flavored tobacco and little coal pellets used in *chillums*. Her customers had become worried. In the winter, summer, or rain—in whatever weather, without fail—Amiran always came out at sunrise to make her rounds of the city, carrying her special tobacco and coal pellets in a little basket for her few select customers. These customers, holding plates or puffing on their *chillums* to keep the coals burning, always came out of their homes to wait.

Using her stick for support and holding the basket on her waist, the tobacco seller would come with her old, worn-out flapping

---

[*] See glossary

shoes, dressed in brown, puckered pajamas, green kurta, and an ocher-colored cloth over her head for modesty. After she approached one of her respected customers, she would lean on her stick a moment to catch her breath and put her basket down on the customer's steps. With her crooked, trembling, ring-studded fingers, she would straighten out the white hair that had become entangled by the morning breeze in her half-dozen tiny, silver earrings. Her tongue would push a ball of finely ground *paan* to one side of her mouth, and she would try to clear her throat. Then snapping her fingers, with a kind of rough but controlled voice, she would call out: "The time for my beloved to return has arrived; I am waiting, standing by the door."

Afterward, she would sell her a few paise worth of tobacco and coal pellets.

Her songs and antics made her customers smile. Once in a while, one of the more elderly might blurt out, "It's a good thing you're too old for romance. Otherwise people would certainly be suspicious of you."

Pretending to be scolding him, Amiran would answer, "Oh, come on, you may have become old, but you still haven't grown up? The truth is that the people we should be most suspect of are those who are old enough to be beyond suspicion."

"If you will make a rule like that," another man would tease, "you certainly will not be beyond suspicion."

Amiran would shoot back, "Don't worry about us women. We're experts on avoiding the path of suspicion." The man would have no alternative but to blush and laugh. Then she would go off down her lane.

The less mature in the crowd would say, "She's shameless." Those a little older would say, "She's frank." And the old men would say, "She's from another world." But if you were to ask Amiran herself, she would say, "What I was before is all dead, and what will happen in the future, only Allah can say. But what am I now? This I know." And then, if someone would press, "Ok,

66

so tell us, what are you?" a strange seriousness would spread over her face, and very softly she would utter, "I'm a *bhairavi* who goes from house to house awakening the spirits."

(2)

The painter's wife, Krishna Priya, had also woken up in the room adjacent to the veranda, and lying on her mattress, she was humming, "Wake up, Krishna, all the birds are singing."

It had become morning. Ram Dayal had the feeling that someone was knocking at the door. He called out to his wife, "Listen to me, dear one. Get up, open the door. Perhaps Amiran has come."

"You spend the whole night as if dreaming about Amiran," she said as she got up, went to the veranda, and peeked into the lane. Seeing no one, she said, "Do you think Amiran has become so weary of life that she'd go outside in the midst of this massacre?"

"Of course, you're right," the old painter said, "but what can I do? This addiction is a bad thing. Look around and see if any tobacco's fallen somewhere. Whatever you find give to me."

"It's all gone by now. You look, if you want," she said. Then she added, "Because of the riots, all the neighbors have run away. Otherwise, I'd go early in the morning and ask them for some."

The helpless Ram Dayal listened to his wife, and even though he knew he would not find what he wanted, he nonetheless started to grope in one corner. Instead of finding what he was looking for, his hand fell on a picture he had once drawn. As soon as his hand touched the painting, he again felt the same burning sensation he had experienced 27 years before, when he was accused of stealing that very painting and had to suffer the trial by ordeal of touching a red hot iron ball to prove his innocence. He immediately pulled his hand away from the picture, but the simmering fire flared again. He looked through the smoke of his memory.

67

There is a thatched hut on a hillock overlooking the Yamuna River. A boy of about 12 or 13 is engrossed in trying to draw the picture of a girl. He is using a little piece of charcoal on the whitewash of a hut. The boy has been hungry for the last 12 hours, but standing in front of the picture, he has forgotten his appetite. Sharp sunlight is blazing on his back, but he doesn't notice that. Then, a seven- or eight-year-old girl appears. She is as determined to scamper over the blazing sand, heedless of her scorching feet, as he is to paint. She is carrying a *lota* full of buttermilk in one hand, and in the other, there are two thick chappatis, some salt, and other spices folded into a leaf. She stands behind the boy, and says in a commanding voice, "Hans, first eat, then draw the picture."

The boy was startled. Seeing the girl, he said, "If your father knows about this, he won't let it go without a thrashing."
Kinkini burst out laughing. She said, "Father had finished eating and was reading the *Nag Leela* in the courtyard. When I saw he was busy, I came over. Why are you wasting your time? You won't be able to draw a picture of me." She put the chappatis, the leaves of spices, and the lota down in front of him. Then she asked, "Why are you so afraid of my father?"

"My father warned me that poor people should fear rich people," Hans said.

Kinkini laughed again. "That's the reason you never come to our house?" she asked.

"Yes," Hans said, his head bent. Fixing his shining eyes on Kinkini's face, he said, "I'm definitely going to finish your picture."

"Good, but first eat." Kinkini continued the conversation while Hans started to eat. "So, when I get married and have my own house, you can come over. You will come, won't you?"

Hans said, "Yes, of course."
Kinkini kept talking, "Since your father died you've been left here alone. I'll see to it that you'll be taken care of. I'll have one of

those large mansions built on the shore of the river. Mango groves will be in front, and behind there will be a flower garden where I'll catch butterflies and you'll draw my picture. OK, now sit down and draw my picture. But first tell me why your father forbid your coming to our house?"

Hans answered a distracted "Yes, of course," to each of Kinkini's questions, including this last. He really did not know the reason. He didn't know that his poor father, unable to bequeath more than his family name, Paramhans, had approached Kinkini's father, Numbradar to suggest that they arrange a marriage between their children, thinking that his fine lineage was enough to offer from his side. But Numbradar, drunk on his wealth, rejected the proposal out of hand. When he returned home, Hans' father instructed his son never to cross the threshold of Numbradar's house again.

Hans finished eating. He stood up to go to the river, get some water, and clean the lota. Before he could do so, however, Kinkini took it and ran down to the water's edge. She quickly got some sand and scoured the lota, filled it with water, and was about to return. Just then, a large, well-built man jumped from a solitary boat. With one hand, he covered Kinkini's mouth, and with the other, he grabbed her waist and lifted her into the boat. The lota fell. A few minutes later the boat set off.

Standing on the hillock, Hans saw Kinkini's abduction. Suddenly, he heard footsteps coming behind him. He heard her father, Numbradar, saying to his servant, "Ram Dayal, hit him so hard on his legs he'll be lame the rest of his life. Forget that he's just a boy." Already familiar with Ram Dayal's cruelty, Hans fled into the nearby forest. He ran and ran for several miles, until he fell down exhausted. There, about an hour later, a traveler lifted him up and asked his name. In a daze, Hans said to the man, "My name is Ram Dayal."

No one in this village ever heard a word again about Kinkini. Hans was gone forever.

3

"What are you staring at?" the painter's wife asked.

"Nothing." He was lost in his thoughts, but he didn't move his eyes from the corner where he found the picture. The eye of his memory was producing different scenes in his mind, and the innate painter within him was beholding their artistic quality.

The court of the Nawab, Askari Mirza, as usual, was drowned in the sounds of nightingales and the fragrance of flowers. Askari Mirza himself was half-reclining on a cushion. On his white hands and feet were the decorations of the red henna design that had been skillfully drawn in the morning. His curly locks were spread on the cushion. Kavavah Fhasih was in front of him, swaying in an opium stupor, and repeating a line from a poem. Next to him stood the poet, Diviaya, dressed formally with a large turban tied around his head. The poet raised his hands in front of him by way of greeting to the Nawab, and said, "Your excellency, I have composed a poem in praise of the beauty of the new begum sahiba. If it pleases you, I will read it."

"Not now," the Nawab said, pointing to the man seated next to him, "This is the artist, Ram Dayal. I had him summoned from Delhi," Mirza said. Then he asked the painter, "I hope your trip was not difficult?"

After receiving the appropriate reply, the Nawab said, "I had you come here to paint a picture of the new begum. You have perhaps heard of her. She is well-known far and wide, even outside of Banaras, for her dancing and singing."

A courtier broke in and added, "She can dance on the edge of a sword, spin as delicately as a top on *batasha*, and move so lightly that a *thali* full of water balanced on her head would not spill a drop!"

"Stop your babbling," the Nawab scolded the courtier. "Come with me," he said to the painter, and the two went into the harem of the palace.

The Nawab was telling the painter, "The begum is very fond of your style. She insisted that if I have a painting done, the talented Ram Dayal must do it." The female attendants in the harem were very surprised to see a man from outside walking with the Nawab in this part of the palace. The Nawab said to one of his attendants, "Tell the begum that Mr. Ram Dayal has come. With artists there is no need to worry about *purdah.*"

When the begum heard the news, she hurried to see the painter. But at the moment she looked at him, she was stunned. "Hans!" she said.

The painter was also shocked. "Kinkini," uncontrollably tumbled from his mouth. The two stared at one another. The Nawab asked, "Have you two met before?" Ram Dayal kept silent.

"Yes, and no," the begum said getting hold of herself. "Yes, once before we met. No, because I didn't know him as the master, Ram Dayal."

"What is this about Hans and Kinkini?"

"That's the name of a melody," the begum said laughing. "That's why even though we only met once before, we managed to recognize one another so quickly. I sang this *Hans-Kinkini song.* In the song, Hans jokes that if a bell-like Kinkini is tied to the foot of a swan-like Hans, then the swan will certainly become the easy prey of a hunter."

"Oh!" the Nawab said.

"Oh!" escaped from the painter's mouth as his wife was shaking him from behind.

"Oh, my god," the painter's wife said, "the Muslims are tearing down the Hanuman temple south of the mosque. After that, they'll attack us. I said right from the beginning that we should have left this place."

"Why are you making such a racket?" the painter said irritably. "For the last 27 years I haven't gone out. How can I face the world now?"

4

"The General Sahib has come along with his British and native soldiers. Now we'll be saved," the painter said to his wife with a sigh of relief.

The painter's wife understood that "General Sahib" really meant Bird. As soon as the British district magistrate, Mr. Bird, arrived, the rioters fled. He looked upward at the old couple standing on the veranda. Understanding that they were not able to flee because of their condition, he felt responsible for providing them a protected place. He approached the veranda, and started to try to convince Ram Dayal to go elsewhere for a few days. To this, Ram Dayal had only one answer, "Sahib, I haven't been out of this house for 27 years. At my age, I'm not able to change." Bird gave up and went away.

The painter's wife started to laugh at her husband. "Why don't we go? The sahib was trying to explain it to you. Why die an untimely death?"

"Nobody dies before his time," the painter insisted, with irritation. "If I were to die before my time, then I would already have been killed by the hands of Mirza Askari, and for 27 years I wouldn't have been hauling around the blemish of theft."

"But you didn't steal the picture."

"For so long, I too thought that I didn't steal the picture; but lately I have started to consider that whatever I did had the stamp of my own meanness on it."

"You've never said that before."

"What I did wasn't so wonderful. I never wanted to tell you about it. Just thinking about it makes me sad."

"But still..."

"Be quiet."

Ram Dayal could quiet down his wife, but not his own mind. He repeatedly said to himself, "Why don't you tell her that....

That the one who sells the coal pellets and opium-flavored tobacco is your childhood friend, Kinkini. Under her old name of Amiran, she was once a famous dancer of Kashi. Because of her charm and beauty, the Nawab, Askari Mirza, made her one of his begums. But one dark, rain and lightning-filled night in the month of January, she was dismissed from the palace. Her only crime was that she had recognized a friend from her childhood, that she had been attracted to his art, and that, in spite of the finished picture belonging to the Nawab, she considered it her own, and gave it to the painter as a reward for his work. When you accepted this, you destroyed Kinkini for the second time. When the Nawab found out what had happened to the painting he said in a large, public audience, "Even after becoming a begum, she still has the mentality of the bazaar." Then the Nawab made Rishishvar Bhatt the owner, and charged you with the crime of stealing the picture. Your conceit did not let you see the truth. You refused to take the blame for stealing the picture, your hands got burned, and you stayed hidden in your house for the rest of your life. Now tell her, tell your wife everything. It will lift some of your burden.

Ram Dayal wasn't able to scold himself the way his wife did. On the contrary, like a criminal, he said to himself, "If I had known, I wouldn't have come from Delhi." Then his mind stopped him.

It wasn't a mistake to come here. You made the mistakes after you arrived. When you went to the Nawab after you finished the picture, and when the Nawab said, "The begum is so white, why did you make her this color?" Why couldn't you just have stayed silent? Or if you had to say something, why did you have to say that the color indeed was not white, but that only a *Vaishnava* Hindu could appreciate the joy and grace that comes from the combination of sky blue and light saffron with brown. That was your first mistake. You made the second mistake when you accepted the picture from Amiran. When you were discussing it,

73

you didn't realize that the most senior wife of the Nawab, Multani Begum, was overhearing your every word.

All these memories were pouring into the painter's mind. He recalled coming for the first time to the begum at night, according to prior arrangement, when they thought they were alone. As soon as she saw him she said, "You have really developed your art, Hans. Do you remember the promise you made to me when we were children?" As she was talking, her voice suddenly choked. Full of feeling she said, "See how strange things are! The love of a woman elevates a man, but the love of a man degrades a woman."

Kinkini was spectacularly beautiful. She was the perfect model for an artist to sacrifice himself. Hans, staring at Kinkini in the splendid light of a one hundred-candle chandelier, silently took a step forward. Kinkini moved two steps back and said, "Don't come any closer. You're tempting catastrophe. I'm being closely watched."

Hans spoke, "I don't care what danger there is." He again moved forward. There was some laughter from outside the door. Kinkini raised the picture and gave it to Hans, "Take this, and get out of here quickly." Hans took the picture and disappeared through a hidden door.

As he was thinking about this, the image of the senior wife, Multani Begum, came to his mind. There were many features of her that were beautiful, but they were all overwhelmed by her obesity. Thinking about her puffy chin and underlip, and her beefy cheeks, Ram Dayal frowned with hatred. His thumb started examining his sharp fingernails, and he said aloud, "If Multani were in front of me right now, I would tear her eyes out, or if not her eyes, then I'd tear her face apart."

The Vaisnava painter looked extremely tormented. This was only the second time that the painter's wife had ever seen this side of her husband in 27 years together. She was frightened. Someone

74

started to knock on the downstairs door, "Open the door. I'm Multani."

Multani came to Ram Dayal. She was an 11- or 12-year-old, scruffy-looking girl, wearing a filthy *kurta* and *pajamas*. Like a parrot, she kept repeating, "Amiran is very sick. She says she only has a few more breaths left. She asks why you haven't ever come to her house? Amiran says that I should tell you clearly that she means her own house, not a house from which someone can abduct her."

"You are very brave, Multani, to come out even in these riots."

"What's so brave about that?" Multani said, "There are people in the streets. Of course, in the lanes here and there are fights. But my name is not Multani, it's Rakiya. I'm the daughter of Nanhay Khan."

"But you said that you were Multani."

"Oh, Amiran calls all wicked women and mischievous girls Multani. Because of my manners, she gave me that name," said Rakiya, alias Multani.

Ram Dayal quietly got up. He put a ragged cloth on his shoulders and groped for his wooden stick, then said to Rakiya, "Let's go."

Krishna Priya, the painter's wife, had been quietly sitting and watching everything. But she could hold herself no longer. She stood up, grabbing her husband's hand. "Where are you going?"

"Amiran's house," Ram Dayal said, choking. Krishna Priya stared at her husband's face for a while and then let go of his hand. Ram Dayal left, putting one hand on Rakiya's shoulder, and with the other tapping his way out of the house using his cane.

Every step of the way, he stumbled. He came close to falling often, but went on anxiously. Suddenly, the slogan, "Allah be praised, Allah be praised" reached their ears. Rakiya froze and stood close to Ram Dayal. Meanwhile, about a dozen men surrounded them. Ram Dayal said to himself, "Now I will surely

75

die. If only it would have happened a half hour later, I would go with pleasure."

"He's kidnapping a Muslim girl. What are you waiting for? Beat him!" one rioter said. A second rioter grabbed the little girl's hand and pulled her away from Ram Dayal. With his support removed, Ram Dayal fell face down. He broke his nose and his remaining teeth. His face was bloodied.

Suddenly, the rioters fled. A well-built youth with a sword had attacked them, and with some help coming up behind him, he managed to frighten them away. The young man said to the wounded painter, "I'll help you get to where you're going. I'm Prasad Narayan, the brother of the Maharajah of Kashi."

"God bless you," the painter said as Rakiya came beside him, and he rested his hand again on her shoulder, "I'll go with this girl." The young man went away, and the two started off again.

Soon, Rakiya was helping the painter stand on the threshold of a hut. She said, "You go inside. I'll go to my house next door."

Rakiya went to her house. Ram Dayal stayed on the threshold wondering whether to go in. He heard Amiran inside trying to sing with a wheezing voice: "Even today he has not come to my place."

The strength that had been in Amiran's voice was gone. Instead, there was sadness. Ram Dayal kept on listening,
Oh, my friend, alas, what should I do now?
What other woman has stopped him from coming to me?

She was trying to put more strength into her voice, but all that came was a frightful hiccup. Then he only heard the echo of her words.

Ram Dayal was not able to delay any longer. He rushed in and called, "Kinkini!"

But Kinkini had become silent. Her eyes were open, a victorious smile on her face.

In the room, her voice was echoing, "...coming to me, coming to me..."

76

Muezzin—the person who calls out prayers in a mosque.

Namaz—the principal prayers a Muslim says five times a day.

Har, Har, Mahadev Shambho—"The beneficent one, Shiva, is the greatest of all Gods".

Radha Shyam—Shyam is an epithet for Lord Krishna and literally means the "dark one." Krishna's consort is the goddess, Radha. Just as the followers of Shiva will often invoke one of his many names, so the followers of the other great god, Vishnu, will often invoke one of Vishnu's many names or the names of his avatars or incarnations, one of which is Shyam (Krishna) and his lover Radha. This reference to Krishna is the first of many references in this story that indicates the main character, Ram Dayal, is a follower of Vishnu, i.e., he is a Vaishnava Hindu.

Yawned—Many people believe that yawning allows evil spirits to enter the body through the mouth where they hover in the morning. Finger snapping scares them away.

Chillum—a kind of pipe, often made of clay.

Pan—a mixture of betel nut, lime and other ingredients wrapped in a betel leaf and chewed as a "digestive."

Bhairavi—the female of Bhairava, a horrific form of Shiva central to the mythic history of Banaras. An outsider to conventional society, she inspires awe for both her protective and destructive powers.

Trial by ordeal—a trial described in the Hindu law books (the Dharmashastras) for people suspected of crimes.

Lota—a small, rounded, metal container open at the top.

Chappatis—round, unleavened breads made of whole wheat flour.

Hans—a boy's name and also the word for a gander.

Kinkini—a girl's name and also the word for a small bell.

Nag Leela—part of an account of the life of Krishna (the Krishna Leela). In the Nag Leela, Krishna demonstrates his extraordinary powers by diving into the Yamuna river to wrestle and tame a serpent, a Nag, who is poisoning the waters.

Nawab—a regional Muslim ruler. While this Nawab's name is fictional, the author, by putting the Nawab in Banaras, may be referring to a brief period starting in 1798 when the Nawab of

77

Oudh (Lucknow) was, in fact, situated in Banaras. At the time, he was being held under house arrest by the British who removed him from Lucknow because of his involvement in anti-British activities.

Begum—the wife of a Nawab, also, more generally, a Muslim woman of high standing.

Batasha—a large, rounded, and very brittle, white sweet.

Thali—a flat, round, metal plate with an edge, at most an inch high, at right angles to the flat surface.

Purdah—the practice of secluding women.

Hans-Kinkini song—a reference to an old form of hunting sport engaged in by Maharajahs. A small bell, a kinkini, was tied to the foot of a wild gander; a hans, the gander released; and then a hunting party would search and hunt it down.

Kashi—"The City of Light," the most ancient of the many names for Banaras.

Vaishnava—refers to Ram Dayal's Hindu worship of Vishnu in the form of Krishna. Colors associated with Krishna are blue, saffron, and brown.

Kurta and pajama—loose-fitting pullover shirt and matching baggy pants.

POSTSCRIPT

Note on Banaras History of this Period

The reference in the story to the British district magistrate, Mr. Bird, identifies this particular Hindu-Muslim incident with riots that began over the *Lat* (staff) of Bhairava in 1809 in another spot in Banaras rife with the symbols of religious conflict. This "staff," originally a 30-foot-or-higher pillar which may date to the days of the Emperor Ashoka (ca 250 B.C.), is considered by Hindus to mark the spot where Bhairava, a form of Shiva, consumes the sins of those who die in Banaras. It is located in the far north of the city and also shares a compound with a Mosque and a muslim martyr's tomb or mazar.

According to British reports of the 1809 incident, tensions started when a Hindu, fulfilling a vow, attempted to replace a temporary structure near the staff with a permanent stone one. This alarmed the Muslim community, fearful that idols would be allowed to stand in their mosque. One side's sacrilege led to a counter-sacrilege by the other, and the violence and destruction escalated until the British authorities regained control three days later. In the incident, the Lat Bhairava was reduced to a stub. In spite of this diminution of physical stature, however, the Lat Bhairava, as a symbol of conflict, is as potent today as ever, as can be seen by the constant police vigil maintained on this spot in northern Banaras.

The Position of Women in India

"The love of a woman elevates a man, but the love of a man degrades a woman."

The Indian cultural ideal of a woman's attitude toward a man (i.e., how a woman's love elevates a man) is captured in the concept of "Pativratya," the faithful, completely obedient and self-effacing wife. In the Ramayana, Sita personifies the virtuous Hindu wife who steadfastly places her dedication to her husband, Ram, above all—following him into exile, and enduring great hardships and temptations for his sake. She remains the model Hindu wife today.

On the other hand, the cultural ideal of men's attitudes towards women, (i.e., how the "love of a man degrades a woman") is more

79

complicated. Although she is venerated in the roles of mother and homekeeper as auspicious and goddess-like, she is also regarded as a destructive and impure force to be reckoned with. Both sides of this attitude have led to a view of women as powerful in benevolent and malevolent ways and in need of control and established limits.

The consequences of this two-sided view can be observed throughout all stages of an Indian woman's life: as a young girl, a married woman, and a widow. A young girl, for example, has the potential to raise or lower a family's or a caste's status aspirations by her behavior. If she is virtuous and can be married into a "better" family, status may increase. However, she can bring shame on her family or caste and their lower status if she goes astray at an early age. Hence, girls approaching puberty—like the heroine of this story—must be closely guarded. Once puberty is reached, even the state of marriage does not prevent the view that a woman's nature contains destructive and impure elements. Menstruation and childbirth, for example, may still cause ritual pollution and be inauspicious to the family. Although these effects are viewed as temporary as long as they are followed by the production of healthy (especially male) children, the impurity takes on a more permanent and devastating quality if the marriage is barren of children. Even if a woman has children and lives "virtuously," her purity is viewed as making her vulnerable and in need of protection from the outside world. One consequence of this is the practice of purdah—the veiling and seclusion of women that is common in north India among Hindus and Muslims. Purdah can take many forms: wearing a burka, the all-enveloping garment worn by some Muslim women outside of the home; covering the head with the end of a sari, practiced by Hindu women when men are present; and staying in the "ladies" compartment on Indian trains and other public accommodations, to mention a few.

Finally, even widows cause concern, especially among the higher castes where orthodox practice is more widely accepted. Because remarriage of widows is not usually allowed among these castes, widowhood that occurs in the childbearing years is likely to be seen as the source of monthly menstrual pollution without the beneficial potential of producing a child. Furthermore, even older widows are considered inauspicious as they have suffered the great misfortune of surviving their husbands. Hence, it is not surprising that the mere presence of a widow can cause concern. For example, in Banaras a fear of the power of widows as a source of bad luck is expressed in the following popular couplet:

> *Widows, bulls, stairs, and Sannyansi*
> *If you can save yourself from these,*
> *for you awaits the liberation of Kashi.*

This couplet suggests that widows are a strong source of distraction from achieving the spiritual liberation that Banaras offers, on a par with the dangers of being gored by bulls, falling from the irregularly constructed stairs of the ghats, and being deceived by phony ascetics.

The suspicion that awaits an Indian woman who cannot conform, for reasons beyond her control, to the high standards of purity demanded by the men of her society is reflected in the character of the heroine of this story. Perhaps it is the author's intention to draw attention to his society's attitudes: on the one hand idealizing women, but, on the other hand, so ready to suspect them of behaving improperly.[1]

---

[1] For further reading about women in India, Michael Allen and Soumyendra Nath, eds, *Women in India and Nepal*, Canberra, Australian National University, 1982.

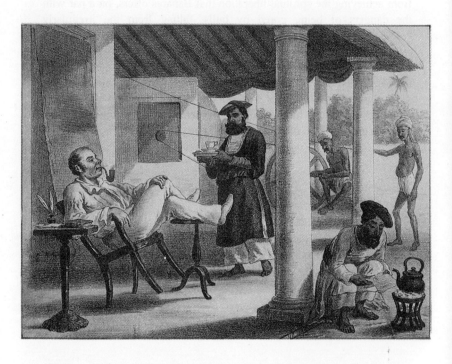

Figure 6.—"Our Colonel" captures some of the flavor of the British imperial presence in India that led, among other things, to the resentment manifested in the Sepoy Rebellion of 1857. This sketch appeared in *Curry & Rice, or The Ingredients of Social Life at "Our Station" in India*, by George Francklin Atkinson.

6

HOW GRAND IS THY MOSQUE, OH LORD

Introduction

This story is set against the 1857 Sepoy uprising in Banaras, a revolt by Indian soldiers in the British army—sepoys. Though the actual fighting in Banaras was short-lived and contained to a small area, the British residents in Banaras, nonetheless, must have felt that much had changed by the time the uprising was over. As one British clergyman in Banaras wrote regarding the new situation faced by Europeans a week after the first shooting, "A white face was a positive advantage earlier; since this outbreak commenced it has been a mark for the assassin." With regard to relationships with Indians, he wrote a few days later, "The dread of the European soldiers has fallen remarkably on the (Indian) people since the engagement....They think them (e.g., the Europeans) demons in human form."[1] In the month or so following the initial disturbance, the white man did indeed become a demon. He had makeshift "gallows" erected wherever an Indian suspected of rebellious intent was found, and search-and-destroy missions razed nearby villages to flush out sympathizers. The Colonel Neill referred to in the following story was the officer in charge of Banaras, and he is often blamed with suppressing the uprising in the Banaras region with excessive enthusiasm. One historian has written about him that, "His name had become a byword for terror, and under his stern authority

---

[1] Both of these quotes were from the letters of the Rev. James Kennedy reprinted in Charles Ball, *The History of the Indian Mutiny*, reprinted, New Delhi, Master publishers, 1981.

large numbers of prisoners, mostly civilians, were executed every day."[1]

Much of the historical record of this period comes from personal letters sent from soldiers and British residents in India to family back home. In contrast to this heavily documented British experience, almost nothing exists to portray the Indian side of the rebellion. In the following, the author ironically uses a letter from an English soldier to his fiancé back home as a device to tell the Indian story. This insider's use of the outsider's perspective is perhaps an attempt to right the historical balance.

The title is taken from a type of folk song called a kawali which is typically sung by Muslims.

Some words and phrases in italic type are explained in a glossary at the end of the story. Also, a postscript to this story, found after the glossary, contains more notes on the Sepoy uprising in India and in Banaras.

It was hardly morning at the Raj Ghat barracks of the British Army, camped in the old fort, when a commotion had broken out. A shocking thing had occurred, frightening everyone. The previous night at 10 o'clock, the highest ranking officer, Major Buckley, a hale and hearty man, went into his tent to sleep. But the next morning, he was found slumped over in his seat, dead.

Major Buckley was still quite young, and was a favorite with officers and subordinates alike. It was out of the question that such a happy man—who was due to return home to be married soon—would take his own life. Furthermore, there were no wounds on his body. The cause of his death was a mystery to everyone.

---

[1] John Pemble, *The Raj, the Indian Mutiny, and the Kingdom of Oudh, 1801-1859*, Harvester Press, 1977, p. 180.

The guard who was standing outside his tent that night stated: "The major was very cheerful last night. He had had quite a few drinks, and was singing, 'When Sally Comes Into The Garden' with a very slurred voice. Once, he came out and said to me, 'I'm going to write an important letter. Don't disturb me when you make your rounds.' Then, he went inside and started to write the letter. Just after midnight, a voice came from inside saying 'Clara, Clara,' and there was a thud from something falling. Then it was quiet again. I thought that maybe, in his intoxication, the major had fallen out of his bed and then quietly had gone back to sleep."

The major's colleagues were seated around the dead body. The army surgeon, having completed a post mortem, had just announced that the major had died of a heart attack. Captain Gower, maintaining a sad expression as far as possible, said: "In this tragedy the one good thing is that he didn't have to drink the bitter cup of the betrayal of his future wife."

Lieutenant Hill's dull eyes met Gower's and, in a surprised voice, he asked, "Is that so?"

"Yes," Gower said, "today I received a letter from a friend, a Member of Parliament. He married Clarisa Keating."

"We should read the letter the major was writing when he died. Perhaps we'll find the reason for his heart attack," the army surgeon said. Gower gave his approval. Hill took the letter from the table and, pausing every now and then, started to read: "Fort Raj Ghat, Banaras, September 1858."

"Sweetheart, I received the letter you sent via Father Moniyar of the Wesleyan Mission when I was in Madras. When it came, I was just about to leave with Colonel Neill for north India. After receiving your long-awaited letter, you can imagine how badly I felt that I didn't have the leisure to open it. Still, I kissed it. Again and again, I kissed it. But like Keats, I also am unable to know if the number of kisses was four or a score. Right

85

now the east wind is blowing, and I am kissing it. Perhaps you will receive them.

"In spite of living in this hot country, I am happy and healthy. The rebellion has been completely suppressed. Under the pretext of punishing the rebels, we are teaching the Indians a lesson they won't forget for hundreds of years. Colonel Neill is truly a very courageous man, and he's shrewd as well. He's had hundreds of gallows built on both sides of the road. Then, he and his troops have been going out with thousands of pieces of rope. Whenever they spot a native, he's a goner. Whether he's young or old, they take him, and tie his hands behind his back with one piece of rope, and with another, hang him by the neck from a tree branch by the side of the road. It's actually quite amusing to watch. For five minutes, up there in the air, there's this fantastic dance and we below are giving three cheers 'In honour of old England.' Try to imagine and enjoy this scene like me.

"Colonel Neill has just left me with a part of the regiment and has gone off to Calcutta. We stay in a ruin, which the local people still call a fort, outside of Banaras. This city, one of the oldest in India, is really quite strange. Hindus regard this city with more respect and reverence than Muslims have for Mecca, Jews and Christians for Jerusalem[*] or Christians for Rome. A civilian friend of mine said that the residents are really quite odd. They just smile with a knowing look about really serious matters, and fight to the death about really small things.

"Take, as an example, something that happened last week. The corporal of my regiment, Bliss, sneaked into town. It very often happens that the troops flee the barracks to go into town for the night. It's against orders, but we officers consider it unfair not to allow this to go on. Human nature should be allowed some leeway. At any rate, the next morning Bliss got lost somewhere inside the old city.

---

[*] These tales predated the creation of Israel.

86

"One thing you should know is that here the lanes are very narrow, very dirty, and quite circuitous. So, Bliss entered one of these lanes and saw a shop where some sweets were being prepared in a large pot with a kind of syrup. These sweets were smallish, round, yellowish, and spun in circles. A man with a long metal tool kept taking them out and placing them in another pot.

"Bliss was hungry, so he reached in his pocket with one hand to get some money and with the other he took hold of one of the sweets.* With Bliss having both his hands occupied, the sweets seller aimed to hit his head with the iron tool that had been dipped in the hot syrup. Bliss's head was spared, but the tool fell on his temple and cut his ear. If it had been some native that this had happened to, he would have got scared and collapsed right there. Anyway, our Bliss retreated, although I doubt that we could really call it that, and managed to escape out of the trap of those lanes and make it back to the barracks. Unfortunately, afterwards he wasn't able to recognize the lane where this incident happened. If he had, we would have eaten that sweets vendor alive.

"Sweetheart, this letter is becoming quite long. The chances to write are so few. Until now I have written about other people, but now I will write about myself.

"As I've already said, this country is quite strange; and that is doubly true of Banaras. When I came here, I fell into a frightful predicament. Like the ghost of the King of Denmark in *Hamlet* who comes out of his grave, an old woman here in Banaras is restless to get out of her grave. At the stroke of midnight last night, she came out of her tomb in a little mosque that she had built near here; and until 2 o'clock she strolled in the open courtyard of the mosque and sang. I don't understand everything, but the first stanza of the song is very clear:'

---

* See glossary

87

'How grand is thy Mosque, O Lord.'

"Dear Clara, when you read, this do not be surprised. This woman pursues me with all her hate. The day before yesterday, before she became a ghost, I had her killed by a firing squad at six in the morning.

"I will tell you the story of this very peculiar woman. You will then be able to see how foolish native women are in their 'love affairs.' The fact is that they don't even know how to love or to care for love.

"This woman's name was Rakiya, and at the time of her death she was 58 years old. She was also known by the name of Multani. In one of her 'love intrigues,' she ended up losing her nose, and as a result, she has quite a frightening appearance. From what I was able to learn from her, when she was a young woman she had already given her heart to someone. But this man was beyond her reach. Not only was marriage quite out of the question, but she couldn't even appear in his presence. But to tell the truth her independent nature would never allow her to accept the status of a married woman. Still, she must have been very pretty. Many important men wanted to make her their wife. But she rejected all proposals, and with her freedom lived an immoral life.

"You will be surprised to know that, like the *Rani of Jhansi,* she considered the mutiny a struggle for freedom; and she was quite fanatically supporting it. Even though the mutiny didn't have much support in Banaras, we were so weakly positioned here that it caused a lot of chaos. Those of us Europeans who could get away fled in boats to *Chunar.*

"I should mention that there's one other strange thing about this place. In spite of the fact that we run things, there's another man they call their king or Rajah. I heard, but have not been able to find the proof, that the father of this Rajah had several boat-loads of Britishers sunk in the river near his fort. We would have hanged him; but as I said, we couldn't find the proof.

"There was an English merchant's family, the Bentleys, in one of those boats that unfortunately sank. They had hired this Multani woman to be the ayyah or servant for their children. Multani was with this family on that last boat trip, but she was saved. If only once she had mentioned that someone or other had given the order to sink the boats, or that from the shore someone was shooting at the people trying to swim to safety, then our entire objective would have been achieved. We tried all sorts of tortures, but in her stubbornness she only had one answer: 'I don't know why the boat was sunk.'

"We also heard that there was a Hindu priest on this boat by the name of Jhalur. He was caught after a long search. The Hindu priests here are usually very forceful and talkative, but this Jhalur turned out to be quite a sickly and foolish man. He didn't even remember that he was on the boat. We had to give up and let him go.

"But that woman—in every pore of her body, she was a rebel. For her entire life, she lived opposing the conventions of her society, and then she died opposing the British raj.

"In order to welcome members of the rebel army on their way through Banaras, she persuaded the local shopkeepers to prepare sharbat by having sacks of sugar dropped in a well. For this alone, she could have been shot a hundred times. But we were really after bigger fish. So, I kept trying to persuade her that if she'd tell me what she knew about the well-known Narayan Singh, the father of the Rajah, I'd see that her life was spared. When she heard my offer, she didn't even answer, but just stood, smiling. With the nose cut from her face, this made quite a terrible sight.

"She finally started to tell me something about herself one day at noon, and even though soldiers were all around me, the experience still frightened me. It started when I was going about my interrogation, and she filled with anger. Making her satanic face even more frightening, she said, 'What nonsense, Sahib! Put

89

yourself in the place of a woman for a moment, and try to imagine that when you were 10 years old, someone saved your life. On that day you gave your heart to this man and spent the rest of your life thinking of him. At the end of your life, someone tries to get you to testify against your beloved. Now tell me, would you be able to betray him?'

"Who doesn't want to save his own life? I asked.

"I don't know what it must be like in your country, but here, even if some Jahangir had come and said that in exchange for evidence against my beloved, he'd make me his Nur Jahan, I would still dismiss him.'

"I started to laugh when this nonsensical and ugly woman compared herself to Nur Jahan and asked, 'Even to save your life?'"

"What is all this about saving my life? One day it will have to end." She said this laughing like a lioness.

"I became angry at her impertinence, and said, 'Tomorrow your life will end. At exactly 6 o'clock, you will be shot. If you have any wish besides sparing your life, then tell us and it will be fulfilled.'"

"Until today, no wish of mine has ever been fulfilled. There has never been one who could fulfil them, so how can you possibly do it? Still, she said, pointing to a mosque, 'If you can do it, let me live until Thursday night. I had that mosque built with great fondness. But the foolish Mullah denounced it and wouldn't allow the Namaz to be chanted in it, because, according to him, it was built from my illegitimate earnings. Well, that really doesn't matter now. I'm glad I had it built anyway. But let me live a few more days. On Thursday night, it will be *Id* and, staying awake all night, I'll be able to chant the Namaz there myself. After that, you can shoot your bullet at me with pleasure. I have also had my grave prepared in that mosque.'

"Nothing can be changed," I said.

"So then why did you ask what I might wish? Liar! But you should know this; on the night of *Id,* I will stay awake all night and chant the *namaz* in the mosque. You cannot stop me,' she said and then singing, 'How great is thy mosque, Oh Lord,' she was taken away to the jail by the guards.

"The day before yesterday she was shot and buried. Still, as I've already written above, she was seen singing and strolling in the mosque. I got angry at the soldier who first brought me the news, but how can I deny what my ears and eyes tell me?

"Dear Clara, today is *Id.* I am writing this letter sitting in the camp right in front of that mosque. It's almost 12 o'clock. The entire camp is still; the wind is whistling. There's no moon in the sky, but the stars are shining. There, the sentry just struck the twelve bells. And look there, that old, noseless lady is starting to ramble in the courtyard of the mosque. Her annoying, nasal voice is coming into my ears. Oh, what is this? That satan is leaving the mosque, and coming toward the camp. She's coming very quickly. She's reached the door. Perhaps the fool of a sentry has fallen asleep. Clara, Clara, save me! This is serious. Oh my God, she's coming into my room. My blood is turning to water from hearing this song. Make it stop, make it stop. I'm suffocating. Make this song stop. Oh Lord, Thy Mosque...."

GLOSSARY
(in order of appearance in the text)

Smallish, round, yellowish and spun in circles—These are probably jalebee, a favorite Banaras breakfast made of a flour and water batter squirted into boiling oil. After cooking, the jalebees are dipped in a hot sugary syrup, and then set aside to cool and dry.

Took hold—Bliss ritually contaminated these sweets with his touch, making it impossible for the vendor to sell them to others. Bliss clearly does not understand what he has done or why the vendor became so angry.

Rani of Jhansi—one of the most distinguished leaders of the uprising. A widowed queen from the area around Gwalior, about 200 miles south of Delhi. She at first opposed the rebels, but when she learned that the British suspected her of treason and planned to try her, she joined in and distinguished herself as a rebel leader. She died fighting in the struggle.

Chunar—about 25 miles downstream from Banaras, this fort was a refuge for the besieged British during the rebellion.

Sharbat—a popular north Indian drink made with the juice of a fruit, water, and sugar.

Jahangir—the third of the great Moghul emperors of India, ruling from 1605 to 1627.

Nur Jahan—the Persian wife of Jahangir and the real power behind the throne, a beautiful, brilliant, and ambitious woman credited with having set the tone and direction of Moghul administration and cultural life.

Mullah—a Muslim teacher or sage.

Namaz—the principle prayers a Muslim says five times a day.

Id—a festival celebrating the end of the month-long fast of Ramadan and commencing with the sighting of the new moon which may not occur until late at night. Traditionally, a special *namaz* is recited on the occasion.

POSTSCRIPT

The Sepoy Uprising in India and in Banaras

The revolt started on May 10, 1857, when Indian soldiers stationed in Meerut killed their British officers and took over nearby Delhi. This action had been preceded by unrest among the Indian soldiers from the beginning of the year, caused by grievances about pay and promotion and the introduction of the Enfield rifle. To load this rifle, Hindu and Muslim soldiers had to bite off the end of bullet cartridges said to be greased with the fat of (sacred) cows and (defiling) pigs. More generally, discontent had spread throughout India over vague apprehensions about the effect of British rule on Hindu and Muslim society.

Though the rebellion quickly spread over north India; for the most part, the British authorities regained control within months. Delhi, for example, was recaptured in September; while establishing order in some major cities, such as Lucknow and Kanpur, took six more months.

The rebellion in Banaras was even more short lived than in Delhi, starting on June 4th and ending in the middle of July. In the city itself, the main disturbances occurred when the British officers—informed of what had happened in Delhi and elsewhere—tried to disarm their Indian soldiers. Instead of submitting, the soldiers fired at their officers and fled, leaving behind 25 British dead or wounded. Though fear reigned among the expatriate community for another month and a half, little actual fighting occurred within the city after this first incident.

In addition to the 200 British soldiers who were stationed in Banaras at the outset of the conflict, another 150 British civilians—government officials, members of the circuit court, merchants, and clergymen—were also resident in the city. For about a month, these British residents lived in the ornate Mint Building (today opposite the Taj Ganges Hotel and the site of the Cottage Industries Exposition). Giving up their bungalows and living in cramped, hot quarters in fear of imminent attack appears to have been the major inconvenience to the civilian British population in Banaras. They were fortunate compared to their compatriots elsewhere in north India, where the number killed and uprooted was far greater. The relative good fortune of the British in Banaras was perhaps a result of Banaras' situation as a transportation center for troop movements to other places, which meant Banaras was comparatively well protected. Also, the cooperation of the Rajah of Banaras with the British is credited with keeping disturbances in the city to a minimum.[1]

---

[1] Nevill, H. R., *Benares: A Gazetteer*, District Gazetteers of the United Provinces of Agra and Oudh, Vol. XXVI, Government Press, Allahabad, 1909, pp. 210-215.

7

In Every Pore a Thunderbolt of Power

Introduction

In this story, the author puts aside Banaras history, and turns to the rich Banaras tradition of folklore. In the following, the monkey god, Hanuman, plays an important role—appearing magically, changing form, and sharing his fantastic strength with a devout follower.

*Some words and phrases in **bold** type are explained in a glossary at the end of the story. Also, a postscript to this story, found after the glossary, contains notes on Hanuman and Banaras, Tulsi Das, and Dattatreya and Pativrata: the faithful, obedient Hindu wife.*

Godavari felt ashamed at the very thought of appearing naked in front of the god.

But what alternative did she have? She wanted to kill herself by hanging, but didn't have any rope; and the only substitute was her sole sari. If she used it, she would be forced to appear naked in front of the picture of the Bal Brahmacharya Hanumanji on the ochre-colored wall.* But this would make her sin even greater than that of killing herself. She stared intently at Hanumanji for a while, and then decided that she couldn't go through with it. Jumping into the lane below from the roof would certainly be preferable.

Seizing on this idea, she went to the roof. Climbing to the edge, she peeked down into the lane. With a shudder, Godavari had to look away; and doing so, her gaze fastened on the flowing Ganges. Godavari realized that drowning was a better alternative and was surprised that such a simple method of suicide hadn't occurred to her before.

The poison of loneliness had gradually permeated Godavari's life to such an extent that with each breath she started to inhale bitter despair and exhale the stench of hatred. She clearly felt that a life without any satisfaction of love, respect, or wealth was really death; and that ending such a life would really be living. She was one of those married women whose life was actually more unbearable than a widow's; this was why she decided to commit suicide. First, she had wanted to take some poison, but she could not find any. Without even one yard of rope, she wasn't able to hang herself. Jumping from the roof was terrifying. So, she went off to drown herself in the Ganges.

It was a January morning. Dense clouds hovered in the sky, hiding the sun; and a stinging, cold wind was blowing as

---

* See glossary

Godavari reached the Ganges shore. Because of the extreme cold, only a few of the usual ritual bathers could be seen scattered on the ghats, and the pandas had set up only a few of their umbrellas. But Godavari went in search of a more isolated place. Passing by the Dattatreya Temple, she climbed down the stairs of Bhosala Ghat. She saw only two men there and decided to wait for them to go. Godavari sat on the last step and hung her feet in the water.

(2)

Jitu *Keyvat* was standing waist-deep in the Ganges. He had been placing handfuls of the riverbed into a sieve and straining out the solid material. He had just overturned one sieve on the steps in front of him; and his nimble, experienced fingers started to probe in the pile of stones and pebbles. One of his well-trained fingers came into contact with a piece of metal. It stopped for an instant. Some other fingers came over to help it, and together they raised the piece to his eyes. His eyes quickly assessed the value of this item; and his mouth, twisted with disappointment, said, "Only a worthless coin."

"What's the matter, Jitu?" Nanaku Ghatiye asked. He tightened the blanket around him and adjusted the checkered towel over his head.

Tucking the coin in his ear Jitu grumbled, "Guru, I don't know whose face I saw when I got up this morning. I can't even find a five-*paisa* coin and I'm all shrivelled up in this freezing cold. But I can't give up; for the sake of my stomach I've got to keep looking."

"Maybe you ought to get out of the water. With these winds and the sky so dark, you'll get sick. The pilgrims don't even come out today. I should be home myself, but I've got to wait for Babu Shivanath Singh. He's a regular client of mine; but even he doesn't seem to be coming, so you should surely get out of the water," Nanaku explained sympathetically. But by then, Jitu was

97

distracted, looking toward the east at a boat dancing on the waves like straw. Clearly the rowers were having trouble keeping it under control, trying with all their strength to bring it into the shore.

With his eyes fixed on the boat, Jitu dismissed Nanaku's imprecations, "Once you place your head on the mortar, there's no point in worrying about the blows that'll follow." Nanaku was about to respond, when Jitu's eight-year-old daughter, Machiya, called out, "Hey, Daddy, if there's a fish, I get the head!" Then, Jitu's son, Jhingava, shouted, "No Daddy, I get the head." Machiya and her brother came running and stood on the ghat stairs in front of their father.

Jitu took his eyes off the boat, faced his children, and said, "When I'm in the house your mother makes my life impossible. When I'm out of the house, you two come and pester me. Life is full of burdens."

Jitu's eyes were dancing with mirth, but the harshness of his voice scared Jhingava whose smile had vanished. Machiya, however, was on to the joke. She broke out laughing and then pulled a large fish out from under her sari. "We'll eat the fish's head, not yours, Papa," she said.

Looking at the fish, Jitu's mouth watered, "Machiya, where did you get such a large fish?"

"It came from uncle's house," she said, full of pride for her uncle's achievement.

Jitu also felt good. "Go, and tell your mother to make this in a curry," he ordered the children. "Get going now." The two went off.

The boat, tossed by the waves, approached the ghat. Jitu said to Nanaku, "We're all set for good food, Guru. Now all I need to find is some decent coin in this mud, and we'll be set for drinking, too."

The boat had arrived at the shore. A passenger, from Bengal, asked his boatman, "Where's Jhalar Thakur's house?"

Godavari, her legs knee-deep in the water, had been waiting for the ghat to empty of Jitu and Nanaku. The cold wind was blowing on her body, but the heat of the fire in her heart made her oblivious to any discomfort. Overhearing Jitu and Nanaku at first gave her some relief that she wasn't the only one who suffered in this world. Then, picturing Jitu's household with husband and children, her feelings of relief were blunted and replaced again by the bitterness of jealousy for the good fortune of this unknown boatman and his wife. She was thinking of getting up and looking for a more isolated ghat, when she heard the traveller who had just arrived in a boat mention her husband's name: "Jhalar." Instead of leaving, Godavari quietly remained.

She heard Jitu telling the traveller, "Not Jhalar Thakur, but Jhalar the moneylender."

Then Nanaku said, "The boatman had it right. In Bengali *thakur* means *Panda.* You don't know these things?"

"Come on, what do you think? I don't know him?" said Jitu. "Since childhood, we've played games on the ghats together. Sure I know him. I can't believe you said that, Guru." This insult to Jitu's knowledge upset him.

The newly arrived traveller asked Jitu again, "Do you know Jhalar Upadhaya Thakur?"

"Who doesn't know him? Everyone knows him," Jitu said, and then began describing this Jhalar Upadhaya, "Arms and legs like twigs, small head, lifeless face."

When she heard Jitu describe her husband, Godavari recalled how simple-hearted and weak her husband was. Because of his innocence and frailty, he was the butt of many a Banarasi joke and prank. People slapped him, and the poor soul just scratched his head and looked around him for the assailant. Or, he might be walking along, and someone would trip him—he'd just come home quietly brushing the dust off his clothes. Even at home, men would insult him and women would ignore him. Godavari, hearing how people made fun of her husband's incompetence, stupidity, and weakness, became inflamed. Just hearing this, and from a stranger's mouth no less, opened her old wounds again. She heard the Bengali traveller saying to Jitu, "No, no, the Thakur I'm looking for is not weak. Oh no, he's a tower of strength."

"Oh, you're talking about after he saw Hanumanji. I was talking about him before that time," Jitu said.

Then Nanaku's voice filled with admiration: "It was Jhalar's habit not to eat until after taking the *darshan* of Hanuman in the *Sankat Mochan* temple. It happened that two years ago in the month of *Shravan,* there was a *solar eclipse.*[*] Because he was so busy making the rounds with pilgrims that day, Jhalar forgot to take Hanuman's darshan. He was exhausted after a full day and came home at nine o'clock. He bathed and sat down to eat. But, just as he raised the first morsel of food to his mouth, he remembered what he hadn't done. He stopped his hand before the food got to his mouth, and said to his mother, 'Watch my plate! I'll be back quickly.' His mother tried in vain to stop him from leaving the house and heading for Sankat Mochan temple. You know, sir, that Sankat Mochan Temple is about three miles from the city. Even in broad daylight, no one has the courage to go there alone. On the way there's Ramapura where the *doms* usually carry out their robbery. The temple is surrounded by dense jungle. Not only frightful animals, but also poisonous snakes and scorpions abound there. On the way, there's the horrible Assi stream. In the rainy season it's so rough that if an elephant happens to fall in, it'll get torn to pieces. And listen to this, sir—it was pouring rain that moonless night. Imagine, the weak Brahmin set off in those conditions towards that very temple. So, rain was falling, and time and again lightning struck, which was good because it provided some light for the Brahmin, who was running

---

[*] See glossary

100

toward the temple unhindered like a *sacrificial horse.* **Whenever he would become frightened he would shout:

"To a forest of the wicked, he is like a raging fire; To the dark cloud of Ram, he is a peacock dancing with love. In every pore of his body is the strength of a thunderbolt; Long live the son of Kesari.

"And then he would go on his way with redoubled speed. Running as fast as his legs would carry him, he reached the bank of the Assi stream, which had become a raging flow. Not seeing any way to cross, he took off his *dhoti* and *dupatta* and hung them on the branch of a tree. He tightened a towel above his *langoti* and prepared to jump. But, he was prevented from doing so when someone grabbed his hand from behind. Shaking his hand to free it, Jhalar turned around and saw that he was in the tight grip of a large, well-built man. Jhalar looked at him beseechingly, and the big man asked, `Do you want to kill yourself?'

"No, I'm going to take the darshan of Hanumanji,' Jhalar replied. The stranger motioned in the direction of the fierce stream and said, 'An elephant couldn't stand firm in that current. You'll be washed away'."

"I won't eat any food without taking the darshan in Sankat Mochan. That's my rule,' Jhalar explained calmly.

"Well, then, assume that you have taken the *darshan of Sankat Mochan*, and now return home," the stranger said.

"If Jhalar had only found a way, he would have fled from this person, but the stranger wouldn't let go of his hand. After such a day, he was exhausted. Then, too, the hunger in his stomach was raging like the *fires on Lanka.* Contrary to his timid nature, Jhalar started to shout: 'Just because you say so, I should believe that I've had darshan? Where is Hanumanji?'

"Looking at the weak and innocent Jhalar losing his temper, the stranger smiled and said very softly, `Why don't you just

---

**See glossary

101

consider me to be Hanuman.' Jhalar became completely outraged. It was the first time in his life that he had ever become angry. Grinding his teeth, he said, 'If any common person can claim to be Hanuman, then what does it mean to see Hanuman? If you're Hanuman, then prove it.'

"What proof will you accept?"

"If you're Hanumanji, then show me the form that you showed to Sitaji—"With a body like a mountain of gold, a brave warrior, terrifying on the battlefield," Jhalar said after considering the matter for a while. *

"You won't become frightened?"

"No."

"OK, then behold," the stranger said, and his body started to grow. It seemed as if his head would touch the sky. Jhalar Upadhaya, speechless, shut his eyes and fell at the stranger's feet.

"When he opened his eyes again he found the previous individual standing in front of him. The man spoke again: "Tell me, what do you want from me? Whatever you ask for, you'll get."

"Jhalar recalled an incident from that afternoon when a Panda slapped him and took his money, and Jhalar, as usual, put his tail between his legs and walked away. Thinking about this, suddenly, from out of his mouth, came the words: 'Give me the strength of your little finger.'

"Hanuman smiled again, and said, 'Your present dark age *kaliyug* physique will not be able to stand such strength. Look upward and open your mouth.'

"Like the papihey bird that keeps its mouth constantly open in expectation of rain, Jhalar raised his face and opened his mouth. Hanumanji pulled a hair from his body and threw it in Jhalar's mouth. It was as if an electric current had passed through his body. Running like the wind, Jhalar returned home. He arrived

---

* See glossary

102

and entered the kitchen, grabbed his plate, and started stuffing food into his mouth. When he finished the things on his plate, he started to eat all the leftovers he could find in the kitchen. And when he finished these, he went into the storeroom, shouting, 'I'm hungry! Hungry!' and ate flour, beans, and rice, whatever was in front of him."*

Hearing what Nanaku was saying, Godavari recalled the events of that night. As a result of Jhalar's incredible conduct, people thought he had become possessed by evil spirits. When Jhalar entered the storeroom, they closed the doors; and for the entire night, he kept devouring whatever he could find.

And then Nanaku went on:

"Yes, sir, and so the next morning Jhalar came to this very ghat and leaned on that crooked stone pedestal over there. Until that day, it was completely straight. When they saw Jhalar, the people around here at first thought it was just that old cry baby Jhalar, and some started to call out sarcastically, `Hey, guru, be careful lest your weight crush the stone pedestal.' At that time, Jhalar wasn't really quite himself. So he thundered, 'Oh yeah? Is that what you say?' He pressed his body on the pedestal till it crackled a little and bent. The people watching shouted, 'Oh my god! Oh my god!' and ran away. Jhalar laughed when he saw this and stuck a piece of rock under the pedestal. You can see, it is still supported on that rock today. After this, Jhalar made a fierce sound and hopped and jumped into the flow of the Ganges. Then what happened, where he went—nobody knows."

"I know where he went after that," the Bengali said.

"You know?" Nanaku asked, surprised. Some distance away, Godavari, as if every hair of her body had become an ear, was impatient to hear what the Bengali had to say. He started to speak: "My older brother is the chief minister of the Rajah of Murshidabad in Bengal. The Rajah is also a patron of Jhalar

---

* See glossary

103

Thakur. It was that same month of Shravan two years ago. The morning *darbar* had started when Jhalar Thakur, wearing only a dripping wet towel, entered the darbar and said to the Rajah Sahib, 'I'm hungry.' Not only the Rajah, but all of us standing there thought that the thakur must be crazy. But, in order not to cause him any problems, we thought it best to give him some food and a place to stay. A little while afterward, the storekeeper informed us that Jhalar had taken one and a half *mon* of wheat flour, and had started a fire in a large pile of dung cakes where he was cooking large, thick breads. Hearing this, we all felt certain that the thakur was indeed insane. But the Rajah—who knows how or why he got this idea—summoned his Muslim elephant driver and directed him to have the elephant head in the thakur's direction, and not to obey the thakur when he asked him to stop.

"The elephant driver followed the Rajah's orders immediately. He got on the elephant and approached the thakur, who was eating his food. The thakur signaled the elephant several times, with a *'hoo, hoo,'** that he should not get near him.

"When the elephant didn't stop, Jhalar broke off a large piece of bread and hit the elephant with it. The elephant whimpered, turned, and fled. When the Rajah heard from the elephant driver what had happened, he went to the thakur and asked him to get the rhinoceros out of his garden. He'd been locked in the garden for a year, and the beautiful garden was being ruined. The Rajah begged the thakur to relieve him of this misery and the thakur accepted the Rajah's request. We all went up to a place in the palace overlooking the scene. The thakur kicked down the gate that had been closed for the past year and challenged the rhinoceros. It started snorting at the smell of a human. As soon as the rhinoceros approached him, Jhalar pounced on him like lightening. He stepped on the animal's back feet and lifted him, using his arms to hold the rhinoceros' front feet. Then, he tore the

---

* See glossary

animal into two pieces, easily, like a cloth merchant tears cloth. Afterward, he sat down and started to offer a libation to honor his ancestors, using handfuls of the rhinoceros' blood. He had the Rajah also do a *tarpan* with the animal's blood. Then he bid us all farewell."

Jitu and Nanaku were stupefied listening to the Bengali's tale. Godavari's lifeless eyes also started to shine. Meanwhile, the Bengali asked, "Does the thakur have a son?"

"No, but he has a wife." Nanaku answered.

"Wonderful, wonderful. I must have the darshan of this virtuous woman who has such a god of a husband," the Bengali said, overwhelmed with reverence.

Godavari's chest swelled with pride, her starved self-respect having received nourishment. She took her feet out of the water, and stood up. She climbed the stairs to return to her home.

GLOSSARY

Bal brahmacharya—one who is celibate all his life. With regard to Hanuman, many believe that his celibacy is the source of his great strength and that it must be respected at all costs. Hence, a woman should never appear naked in front of an image of Hanuman.

Ji—an honorific suffix.

Ocher-colored—an auspicious color associated with Vishnu.

Ghats—steps leading down to a river.

Panda—a title for a Brahman religious functionary who administers rituals to pilgrims and residents of Banaras visiting holy places. Here, the term refers more specifically to those who sit under straw umbrellas on the ghats of the Ganges.

Keyvat—a caste name for a boatman. Like many boatmen along Banaras' shore, this Keyvat is skilled at sifting through the riverbed along the shoreline in search of money and jewels. Pilgrims offer these to the goddess Ganges as a religious donation. To make an offering to Ganges, privately without others knowing, is considered highly meritorious.

Ghatiye—a caste name for one who works in one of the stands along the ghats. When residents or pilgrims bathe, they go to these stands and use the services of the ghatiye's to protect their clothing while they are in the river. After bathing, the ghatiye notes in a book that the person ritually bathed that day, lets him use his mirror, and fixes an auspicious mark (tilak) on his forehead.

Guru—a teacher or spiritual guide, and in Banaras, a widely used term of respect.

Face—a popular folk belief in India holds that the first face seen in the morning determines how the rest of the day will go.

Paisa—the smallest monetary unit of the rupee, one hundred of which equal one repee.

Darshan—an "auspicious sight" of a deity's image in a temple, one of the main forms of formal worship in Hinduism.

Sankat Mochan temple—located just off the road that goes from the Durga temple in south Banaras to Banaras Hindu University. Before the 1930s expansion of Banaras, this place was considered a wild area outside the city limits, dangerous to visit after dark.

Shravan—a month of the Hindu calendar that occurs in July/August, in the rainy season after the temperature has cooled somewhat from the hot, dusty preceding months. This is a popular time for pilgrimages to Banaras, and many fairs connected with temples and religious events take place at this time.

Solar eclipse—immediately before and after and during an eclipse, taking food is considered inauspicious. This is a time when the angry demon Rahu is present, symbolized by the disappearance of the sun or moon. Many pilgrims come to bathe in the Ganges to negate the contaminating effects of the eclipse. Hence, a priest who works with pilgrims could be expected to be especially busy on such a day.

Doms—the caste whose work at the cremation grounds of Banaras is considered highly degrading and ritually polluting. Hence, the Doms are much despised by many in Banaras. They are considered capable of the most heinous crimes.

Sacrificial horse—a reference to the Vedic practice, Ashvamedh, of allowing a consecrated horse to wander freely for one year before it is sacrificed. The horse was followed by the King's army, and whatever territory it covered became the King's domain. **Kesari**—a reference to Hanuman's mother that appears in this well known verse by Tulsi Das.

Dhoti—the traditional dress of north Indian men, consisting of a white, ankle-length cloth elaborately wrapped around the waist.

Dupatta—a piece of cloth that often serves as scarf for men and women, but may be also used as a turban or other piece of clothing.

Langoti—a type of G-string or loincloth.

Darshan of Sankat Mochan—because the main image at the Sanket Mochan Temple is Hanuman, "To take the darshan (the sight) of Sanket Mochan," means to see Hanuman.

Fires on Lanka—a reference to the *Ramayana* when Hanuman allows himself to be captured by the demons on Lanka and to have his tail set on fire. Then freeing himself, he grew to an enormous size and leapt from rooftop to rooftop, setting fire to buildings with his flaming tail.

"With a body like a mountain of gold, a brave warrior, terrifying on the battlefield,"—a quotation from Tulsi Das' *Ram Charit Manas* about how Hanuman's body grew big, like a golden mountain to convince Sita that he was no ordinary monkey.

107

Kaliyug—one of the four ages which are passed through serially—Kritayug, Tretayug, Dvaparayug, and Kaliyug. Passing through the yugs is marked by a progressive degeneration in the vitality and morals of man. The present Kaliyug, which still has another 427,000 years to go, is the most degenerate and mankind is at its weakest. It is to this weakened condition of mankind that Hanuman is referring.

Hungry! Hungary!—tremendous hunger is an attribute of Hanuman, and Jhalar's immense appetite implies that he has assumed this aspect of Hanuman. The attribute of always being hungry probably comes from being a monkey. He is supposed to be especially fond of laddu, a round sweet made with the flour of chick peas. Jhalar has also displayed other Hanuman characteristics since being fed his hair, such as his hopping and jumping into the river.

Darbar—a public audience between a ruler and his subjects.

Mon—a standard of weight equal to about 90 pounds.

"hu, hu"—because a Brahmin should not speak while he is engaged in the ritual activity of eating Jhalar does not use words to signal the elephant.

Tarpan—a ritual offering of water, rice, and sesame seeds made for the benefit of one's ancestors or one's family god. Jhalar's behavior, in this somewhat bizarre parody of standard ritual practice, may be construed as acceptable in the context of his state of divine possession.

108

POSTSCRIPT

Hanuman and Banaras

In Banaras, devotion to Hanuman, the monkey god who performs many miracles during the epic the *Ramayana*, can be observed at Hanuman's principal place of worship, the Sankat Mochan ("Liberator of Troubles") Temple. Sankat Mochan is one of the busiest temples in the city and certain to be on many a pilgrim's list of places to visit, in part because the temple's image of Hanuman is believed to have been established there by the monkey god himself. According to one account, Tulsi Das, the sixteenth-century Banaras poet who popularized the story of Ram and the exploits of Hanuman in his vernacular version of the *Ramayana*, one day noticed an old leper attending the daily telling of Ram's story. Having always believed that he would meet Hanuman, Tulsi Das followed this man who, as the story goes, eventually confessed to being Hanuman and disappeared leaving behind the Sankat Mochan image.

Hanuman's character combines selfless devotion and humility with aggressive physical action, tremendous strength, and mental cunning. His boldness and activity are often for the sake of his master, Ram, for whom he has unlimited devotion and love. By extension, Hanuman is also the "Liberator of Troubles" for those who are similarly devoted to Ram. He has many other attributes, as well. In addition to his great strength, he is a fine singer and a scholar of the Vedas. Hanuman can change his size and, as he did in the above story with Tulsi Das, he can change form. This happens also in the preceding story in a reference to Hanuman's rescue of Ram's wife, Sita, who had been abducted to the island of Lanka by the evil demon, Ravana. Hanuman became a giant and leapt across the waters; and then, in order to enter the island, he became a mosquito. When he found Sita skeptical that a little monkey would be able to help her out of her predicament, he increased in size to show her that he was not just any monkey.

Hanuman's magical strength and his other fantastic abilities are attributed to several sources. According to one account, at birth Hanuman thought the sun was something to eat, and so he took it in his mouth. The consequent darkness of the world angered Indra, the king of the gods, who hit Hanuman on the chin in an effort to get him to spit out the sun.

109

This blow so angered Hanuman's father, Vayu, the god of air and wind, that he stopped all the air. In the chaos and panic that followed, all the gods beseeched Vayu to stop his action. In the end, he relented in exchange for all the gods' sharing their powers with Hanuman.

Hanuman's physical strength and purity are honored at akaras, clubs in which physical exercise and wrestling are practiced by boys and men. Hanuman is a kind of patron saint of wrestlers, and many of these akaras are located near Hanuman temples or shrines where homage is paid to the god before the rounds of physical exercise begin.

Tulsi Das

Hanuman's fame and popularity, while linked inherently to the ideal he inspires, are also linked with the popularity of Tulsi Das, considered to be among the greatest of Indian poets. Tulsi Das' influence is especially strong in Banaras and in other parts of the Hindi-speaking regions of north India. In southern Banaras, a popular temple dedicated to his memory attracts thousands of visitors daily; and boatloads of pilgrims plying the Ganges ask to have Tulsi Das' house, now a Hanuman temple on the shore of the Ganges, pointed out. Another enduring legacy of Tulsi Das that brings to mind Hanuman are the annual Ram Leelas. These are enactments of Tulsi Das' story of Ram—staged by over fifty community groups in the city each year. Some of these Ram Leelas have special legendary significance attached to certain episodes such as the Bharat Milap episode (the reunification of Ram with his brother Bharat) that takes place in the area of Nati Imli in northern Banaras. Hundreds of thousands will annually attend this fifteen-minute performance because it is said that Hanuman himself once appeared there—as he appears magically in the story.[1]

Dattatreya and Pativrata: the Faithful, Obedient Hindu Wife

Pativrata, the ideal of the faithful, obedient Hindu wife, is personified here in the person of Godavari, a self-effacing woman almost

---

[1] For a more detailed account of this incident, Lutgendorf, Philip, *The Life of a Text*, Berkeley, University of California Press, 1991, pp. 272-273.

to the extent that she has no existence apart from her husband. Her life without him has become no longer worth living.

The writer reinforces this image of the pativrata at the beginning of the story when Godavari passes by the Dattatreya Temple on her way to the riverbank. The mention of this temple, and especially the image of the three-headed Dattatreya figure inside, creates an association in the reader's mind with an exemplary woman, a pure pativrata, revered for her piousness and celebrated for her loyalty to her husband. Her name is Anasuya. According to the myth, the trickster sage, Narada, went to the wives of Shiva, Brahma, and Vishnu—Parvati, Saraswati, and Lakshmi—and praised the virtue of Anasuya. He told them there was no one else like her. The goddesses became jealous and begged their husbands to tempt Anasuya.

The gods accepted; and disguising themselves as beggars, they visited Anasuya. As she prepared to feed them, they asked to be served by her naked. The dictates of hospitality demanded that she accede to the wishes of her revered guests; but in complying, she sprinkled holy water over them, changing them into babies. She gave them her breasts to suck and kept them in her house as children.

The angry spouses of the gods came to Anasuya and pleaded for the release of their husbands. Anasuya agreed to restore and release them only if each of them would leave a part of himself with her. Accordingly, a three-headed, six-armed child deity was created by the three gods, and named Dattatreya, the central head of which represents Vishnu, while that on the right is Shiva, and the left is Brahma. This is the image in the Dattatreya temple above Bhosala Ghat, near where the story's incident is said to have occurred.

111

Figure 7. A sketch of several wealthy landowners enjoying a hookah from *L'Inde des Rajahs*, by Louis Rousselet, published in 1875.

8

Shivnath And Bahadur Singh, What A Pair!

Introduction

In addition to returning to the glorified past of Banaras' gundas, introduced in the third story, this tale touches on an important and ever-present aspect of life in Banaras: ghosts. While in some cultures, a ghost's appearance might be considered fanciful, in Banaras the presence of a ghost can give a story an added dimension of reality. Indeed, the ghost's shrine referred to in the story is venerated today and the nearby shopkeepers, if queried about its history, will tell this story to explain its origins.

The title of this story is taken from a popular folk song introduced as the story opens. The song is a Lavni, a type often performed in singing competitions in which neighbors gather together late at night during the hot season to sing about local legend and history. Different groups or individuals challenge one another, one side singing part of a refrain and an individual or group of the other side singing the other part.

Some words and phrases in italics are explained in a glossary at the end of the story. Also, a postscript to this story, found after the glossary, contains notes on ghosts in Hindu belief and in Banaras.

Above, in the large *Pipul* tree, the crows started to caw. Below, almost five hundred people were dreamily swaying, singing, and playing music. The *lavni* competition had started at ten in the evening and, now at dawn, was still going strong. Five men were singing in unison even as they hit the *chang:*

"Shivnath and Bahadur Singh, what a pair!

Having come to fight, they would not turn back.

Then a man melodiously and joyfully sang:

Two companies of British soldiers came with their horses.

They blockaded every lane and street.

Their leader, the Mogul Mirza, took his vow to root out

the two villains, placing his hand on the Koran."

At that moment, Fenku pressed the hand of Rupchand, seated next to him, and said, "It's time to go."

This musical event had started, as it always did, five days before *Holi,* north of the Nilkant Mahadev Temple where today the Shiva Temple of Darbhanga-Naresh stands. It was morning, and Fenku was impatient to get going. Two days before, on Mir Ghat, he had got his head bashed in a stick fight. He'd placed a bandage on the wound, but now, because he'd been awake all night, not only did his head ache, but also the wound was throbbing. Rupchand also was tired. So, he quickly accepted Fenku's proposal, and they stood to go home. The two took a few steps south and then turned. Rupchand pointed to the platform in front of them and said, "Look friend, that's the place where someone snatched the dairy cream out of my hand last night."

Rupchand was only a boy of 16 or 17. Recently, he'd moved from his native *Punjab* to *Kashi,* where he settled in the Gharvasi Tola near the center of Banaras. When he heard about the public singing being organized in his neighborhood that night, he left his store; and instead of going home, bought some cream and went toward the Nilkant temple. From the direction of Bhramanal, he turned toward the crossing. Just as he approached there, someone snatched the clay container of cream and fled. He looked around, but in spite of the considerable moonlight, he couldn't see a soul. The memory of this event gave him goose bumps.

His companion, Fenku, was a strapping young 20-year-old. Fenku shook his head and said knowingly, "Oh." For Rupchand, the mystery of the disappeared cream thickened.

The morning light had brightened still more. People had started to return from their bathing in the Ganges and from buying vegetables. Some old women were throwing rice and flowers on a shrine at the crossing. Overhearing Rupchand's story, they turned pale and shuddered with fear from their own memories. Next to them an old man passing by also overheard, and his body tingled with fear.

When Fenku saw all of these reactions, he started to smile. The old man said, "Son, this is nothing to laugh about, this is the shrine of a very brave man."

"Oh, that's Shivnath's, isn't it? I know all about him.
He was born and raised in this very neighborhood," Fenku said pridefully.

Rupchand was looking from his companion to the old man. He asked, "What are you talking about? Why doesn't someone say what this is all about?"

Fenku said, "Let's go home. I'll tell you there."

Rupchand insisted, "No, no. First tell me who this Shivnath was and why this shrine was built."

"If you're so impatient, why didn't you stay for the entire *lavni*? You would have heard more about them in the songs," Fenku scolded.

"I don't understand anything from songs and things like that. Punditji, tell me, who was Shivnath?"

The old Pundit answered:

"Shivnath Singh was a *kshatriya* and a well-known *gunda* of Kashi. Around the clock, he would openly invite prostitutes to dance and sing. He was a skilled gambler, and the sound of *sixes*

115

and nines always echoed in his house. 'No problems with money. Just play a clean game,' was his motto. When people heard his name, their blood would turn cold with fright; and he himself was as bright and strong as the noon-day summer sun. Just like the sun is the answer to the moon, so too, *Babu* Bahadur Singh was the answer to Shivnath Singh—brave just like him, a lion just like him. There's a saying that a horse will only tolerate a kick from another horse. So, too, the strength of Shivnath Singh and the power of Bahadur Singh could only be tolerated one by the other. In order to remove fear from their disciples, they used to divide them into two groups and have them wage a type of sacred war— without animosity or ill feeling for four weeks in the late winter. This really was a sacred war! Father and son would fight, and brother would assault brother.

"People weren't out for each other's weaknesses, like when this head got bashed in," the old man said pointing his finger at Fenku, who had been squeezing the hand of Rupchand and motioning with his eyes that they should get moving. This just encouraged the old man. For his part, Rupchand was as much drinking in what the old man said as listening to him. So, he completely ignored Fenku's hints. The old man started again, "This happened a hundred years ago. The British Raj was still new in Banaras. There were no police then, just soldiers. There wasn't any cowardice either, but respect for manhood. Disputes were not made up, but came of their own accord by challenging those in a commanding position. In the British times, local gambling and country liquor were prohibited, just like today. But in Shivnath Singh's courtyard, two gambling games were always going on. And at the head of each game, Shivnath Singh and Bahadur Singh would stand holding their naked swords in one hand and collecting money and stuffing it in their bags with the other. The door stayed open 24 hours a day. What audacity and authority they had! Even a bird couldn't flap its wings without their permission."

116

The old man stopped and took a breath. Rupchand was bobbing in a sea of astonishment. A terrible wave of fright was washing over him. The old speaker smiled and started again:

"In those days, Mirza Pancu was the head authority for the British here. He considered himself to be another *Lal Khan*. He used to gather up a platoon of soldiers and go out on patrol. He would read the *namaz* five times a day to show that he was a religious man. But, despite all his show of piety and power, as long as Shivnath Singh continued in operation, the man was disgraced. Mirza Pancu and his soldiers had clashed with Shivnath and Bahadur before. Like a wave that breaks into a thousand pieces after it crashes into a rock, he also was confident and strong before the collision; but afterwards he was broken and defeated.

"In the end, Mirza Pancu took up his Koran and swore that he would destroy Shivnath and Bahadur. So, he called together a few battalions of soldiers, about five hundred men, and surrounded the house. Shivnath Singh had gone out, but Bahadur Singh was there, and his hands and legs were shaking. Even the group of gamblers had become worried.

"One of the most active and cunning of the gamblers leapt up and closed the door to protect them. The soldiers started to beat on the gate with the butts of their rifles. To Shivnath Singh, who observed this from outside, this assault was not so much on the gate, as on his pride. Bahadur Singh tried to get up, but the gamblers made him sit down. Meanwhile, outside, a rout had started. People peeking out from behind their windows saw that the soldiers, one after the other, had abandoned their weapons and fled. Here a few were writhing in pain, and there four had fallen dead. Right in the middle of it all was Shivnath Singh—soaking in blood, biting his lips in anger, waving his sword, out of control with rage.

"Seeing this scene from his window, Bahadur Singh was ashamed. He ordered the door opened, but Shivnath said, 'The

117

person who closed that door disgraced me. Only after cutting his head off, will I enter the house.' Hearing the *Thakur's* words, everyone inside started looking at one another. The guilty one, folding his hands, came forward. 'What, it was *you*, Pundit?' The words rushed out of Shivnath Singh's mouth when he saw the old man come forth.

"Yes, *Dharmavatar*," said this Brahmin, who was the *chillum*-filler in the gambling parlor. The Thakur thought for a moment, and then said, 'Get out! Never show your face around here again.'

"The Pundit left with his head hung in shame. Then Thakur Shivnath Singh went inside the house. After bathing and extinguishing the flame of his anger somewhat, he came and sat down in the courtyard. Right next to him sat Bahadur Singh. Neither looked at the other. Then the same Brahmin came running back. Panting, he said, 'Master, two army battalions have come. There are also foreigners among them. Mirza Pancu swore on the Koran that he would either kill or be killed.'

"Shivnath frowned. He got up and went in the direction of the door. Then he thought awhile and said to the Pundit, 'Close the door.'

"The Pundit, smiling to himself, closed the door. Soon the army rushed forward. The house was surrounded. The British soldiers started to shout abuse and shoot.

"For a while things stayed like this. Then suddenly, Bahadur took up his sword, rushed through the window, and jumped to the ground. Seeing this, Shivnath couldn't stay put—he jumped also. What need be said! The two of them showed their swordsmanship so that the enemy was frightened and frustrated. But then, the bayonet of one white man pierced the heart of Bahadur Singh. The bullet of another white man finished him off. Now Shivnath Singh was fully enraged. He began the fight to his death. One of the *Telegu* soldiers struck him on the neck with his sword so that the head, cleanly severed, fell some distance away. For a moment, the soldiers were elated; but in the next instant, they were terrified to see that the headless body kept working the sword as before and continued wreaking destruction."

The old Brahmin stopped his narrative, pointed a finger at Rupchand, and with an intense voice said, "There used to be a *paan* shop right where you're standing. Shivnath Singh usually took his pan there. What was left of him, swinging sword and all, arrived up to there, where the shrine is, and as was Shivnath Singh's custom, his hand reached out toward the pan vendor. 'Oh God' the vendor shouted before fainting. The headless body stumbled and fell."

Rupchand was pale. He was becoming conscious of a faintness himself. Fenku added to the Pundit's narrative, "So from then on, at odd hours of the night, Thakur Singh snatches drinks and food from people who walk by here."

Rupchand fainted. Fenku belched, and then came the weak, sour odor of half-digested cream. Not far away, on the corner of the lane, lavni singers were leaving with the refrain ringing in the air: "Shivnath Singh and Bahadur Singh, what a great pair!"

GLOSSARY
(in order of appearance in the text)

Pipul tree—a sacred tree associated with Vishnu who is said to occupy every leaf.

Chang—a type of drum with cymbals attached.

Moghul Mirza—probably a Muslim official, previously connected with the moribund Moghul empire, whom the British had appointed to keep law and order in Banaras at the end of the eighteenth century.

Holi—a major Hindu festival celebrated in the spring.

Punjab—A state in the northwest of India, part of which was partitioned to Pakistan in 1947. Many of the merchants in the center of Banaras came from Pakistani Punjab after partition in 1947. Like Rupchand, they probably knew little of the local Banarasi traditions before arriving.

Kashi—"The City of Light," the most ancient of the many names for Banaras.

Pundit ji—A name of respect applied to learned people. Often, as in the case of this story, the Pundit is a Brahmin.

Kshatriya—Kshatriya is one of the four varnas or castes. From top to bottom, the four, along with their traditional occupations, are *brahmans* (priests), *kshatriyas* (warrior-kings), *vaishas* (merchants-artisans-landowners), and *shudras* (servants).

Gunda—a hoodlum in modern usage, but previously a neighborhood or district warlord idealized as a warrior correcting the evils of his society.

Sixes and nines—a game in which shells are tossed like dice. Based on the results of the toss, players move their pieces around a board.

Babu—a title of respect or endearment.

Lal Khan—a Muslim general who considered himself to be very righteous and had a reputation for having forcibly converted large numbers of Hindus to Islam.

Namaz—the principal prayers a Muslim says five times a day.

Thakur—a title for a person of the kshatriya, or warrior/ruling caste.

Dharmavatar—the incarnation of dharma, the upholder of the sociocosmic order. This response by the Brahmin reminds Shivnath Singh that to kill the Brahmin is the highest of Hindu sins, one likely to be righted by the Brahmin's ghost. The use of this term also

120

reminds Shivnath Singh that it is the dharmic responsibility of a member of the *kshatriya* caste to protect Brahmins, not to harm them.

Chillum—a small clay pipe used for smoking.

Pan—a mixture of betel nut, lime, and other ingredients wrapped in a betel leaf. When chewed, it mixes with saliva into a bright red color.

Telegu—one of the south Indian languages. Hence this refers to soldiers from the south who were especially favored by the British.

POSTSCRIPT

Ghosts in Hindu belief and in Banaras

In popular Hindu belief, a soul passes through a dangerous intermediary stage between cremation and joining the ancestors. At this undesirable point, the disembodied soul is still attached to this world as a ghost. Banaras is an especially important place for the living to facilitate the transition from ghost to ancestor on behalf of their recently deceased relatives. The city's importance in this regard comes from the relationship between the god Shiva, and the goddess Ganges, and the latter's association with immortality.[1] One manifestation of this relationship is that Banaras is the almost constant scene of service to the ancestors where the ritual, *pinda pradan,* the ritual offering of balls of cooked rice or grain to the ancestors, is performed daily in small individual or group ceremonies at Manikarnika Ghat, the main cremation ground. This ritual, conducted over 13 days, usually ends with the chief mourner pressing a part of a food ball, representing the body of the recently deceased, into the middle of three other food balls which represent three previous generations of relatives. This "mixing" of the recently deceased with the ancestors, encourages the new soul safely into the other world, no longer threatening the living as a ghost.

In certain cases, however, the ghost does not or can not make the transition—for example when an individual has suffered a "bad" death, e.g., a violent, unnatural, or especially premature death, and the proper rituals cannot be performed. When this happens, the deceased must exist in the middle realm as a ghost, benevolent or perhaps malevolent in

---

[1] A King Sagar threatened to take over the throne of the king of the gods, Indra. To stop him, Indra had Sagar's 60,000 sons turned to ashes. Three generations later, a descendent of Sagar, King Bhagirath, after performing greatly austere ascetic feats, won the boon from Brahma of the Ganges coming to earth to revive his 60,000 deceased relatives. Through more ascetic feats, he was able to win a boon from Shiva to reduce the fury of the flow of the Ganges falling from heaven by Shiva's capturing it in his locks of hair so that the earth would not be destroyed. When Ganges flowed over the ashes of the 60,000 bodies of Sagar's sons, they were revived; and in this way, the Ganges is closely associated, from her first moment on earth, with service to the ancestors.

nature. Some become angry and harrass the living, as the ghost of this story appears to have done, or some focus their attentions on a particular individual, who may have to see an exorcist to become free of the spirit or perform rituals and have a shrine built. Other ghosts are considered demigods or deities, endowed with special powers and able to fulfill human desires. Usually these more benevolent spirits are thought to have been heroic martyrs, killed in defense of something about which they had strong feelings.

The significance of these ghost spirits should not be underestimated. A large number of people either fear they will be possessed or actually experience such possession. On every Thursday, for example, hundreds of Hindus and Muslims go to the shrine of a Muslim saint near the main railway station in Banaras and attempt to communicate with their ghost through the medium of the saint honored there. Another way of dealing with ghosts is through their deification visible in the construction of shrines and the worship of the ghost's image. Banaras has hundreds of such shrines to "Bir Babas."[1] Some of these are more popular, especially to lower caste Hindus, than the conventional gods and goddesses. Their deification transforms the forces generated by a violent and tragic death into powers to help the living.

---

[1] Diane M. Coccari, "Protection and Identity: Banaras Bir Babas as Neighborhood Guardian Deities," in Sandria B. Freitag, *Culture and Power in Banaras*, University of California Press, Berkeley, 1989, pp 130-146.

9

Alas,
This is Where My Nose Ring Got Lost

Introduction

*This story brings us to India's independence movement and an
event that took place in Banaras when foreign-made clothes were
collected and burned in protest at the town hall, probably in the 1920s.[1]
This protest act was part of the countrywide boycott described in this
story of British-made goods, especially imported cloth. Wearing clothes
of native Indian* swadeshi *cloth became popular instead. Mahatma
Gandhi added to the movement by promoting village, hand-spun cotton,
known as* khadi *cloth which is sold today in Gandhi Ashram stores.*

*This story is also about the life of a prostitute. That she should be a
talented singer is not surprising, because in the Indian tradition, the arts
of singing and dancing were at one time the exclusive preserve of a
certain class of courtesan, called* ganikas *or* gavanaharin. *In Banaras,
this tradition continues today, in an attenuated form, with the singing and
dancing women who live and work in the second-floor apartments above
one of the city's main bazaars.*

*The title of this story is drawn from a "chaiti," a spring song which
an individual or group may sing in the month of Chait, or March/April.
Chaitis are usually full of appreciation for the romance of springtime.
For example, this story's title is a line from a song in which a young
woman must embarrassingly ask the members of her husband's family if
they have found her nose ring, a symbol of her being a married woman.*

---

[1] Takur Prasad Singh, *Svatantrata-Andolan Aur Banaras,* Vishvadidyalay Prakashan,
Varanasi, 1990, p. 44.

124

This had apparently gotten lost in the previous night's lovemaking with her husband.

Some words and phrases in italics are explained in a glossary at the end of the story. Also, a postscript to this story, found after the glossary, contains notes on folk music in Banaras.

(1)

Dulari was doing her push-ups vigorously, her Maharastran-style sari wrapped around her, bra and underwear pulled tight. The sweat dripping from her body outlined her figure on the ground. When she finished the exercises, she wiped her body with a checkered towel, untied the knot of her hair, and dried it. Afterward, standing in front of a full-length mirror, she turned to admire her strong arms, proud as a wrestler. Then, she started to eat a bowl of chick-peas soaked in water with green peppers and pieces of onion.

Before she could finish her meal, someone was rattling the door latch from outside. Taking off her exercise garb, Dulari dressed properly in a sari, did her hair up neatly, and opened the door.

Tunnu was standing outside with a bundle pressed under his arm. He looked scared, with a trace of an embarrassed smile on his thin lips. With a dismissive rudeness Dulari stared into Tunnu's eyes and said, without any formality, "What, it's you here again? I told you not to come here, didn't I?"

Tunnu's smile vanished. He answered dejectedly, "It was the festival of the year so I thought that..." As he was talking, he took the bundle from under his arm and put it in Dulari's hands. Dulari started to look it over—a hand-spun, cotton sari.

Tunnu said, "This is a specialty of the Gandhi Ashram."

"But why did you bring it to me?" Dulari asked harshly. Tunnu's skinny body seemed to wither even more. Dryly he said, "Didn't I already say that it was *Holi* ?"

125

Dulari interrupted Tunnu, raising her voice, "OK, so it's Holi. Answer me! Why did you come here? Couldn't you find some other funeral pyre to burn yourself on than to come here? What are you to me—my master, my son, my brother? If you know what's good for you, you'll take this shroud and get out of here!" and she threw the sari contemptuously at Tunnu's feet.

Tunnu's eyes—which had a touch of *kajal* over the lower part—started to fill with tears at the insult. "I'm not asking anything from you, am I?" he said hesitantly, bending his head. "Look here, even the stone idol of a god doesn't reject a present brought by a devotee; and you're just a mortal made of flesh and bones."

"Yes, and because I'm just made of flesh and bones," Dulari said, "dogs make my life miserable."

Tunnu didn't answer. Kajal-filled tears were falling from his eyes onto the sari at his feet. Dulari kept on, "You haven't even lost your baby teeth and these romantic ideas chase around in your head. There's a father who works for a pittance all day at the ghats and, with the little he earns, runs a household. And here's his son galloping around on a horse of romance. I'm telling you this for your own good; this street's not for the likes of you. On top of that, you want to have an affair with someone who's probably older than your mother!"

Tunnu listened to Dulari's speech like a statue. He only responded, "There's no way to control the heart. It doesn't take account of age or beauty."

Then he left the room and started to descend the stairs very slowly. Dulari stood looking at him. Her eyebrows were still drawn tight, her face stern. But the softness of compassion had taken the place of harshness in her eyes. She picked up the sari, stained by kajal-blackened tears. She looked again at Tunnu going down the lane, and then began to kiss those stains again and again.

126

Tunnu first entered Dulari's life in Khojwa Bazaar a full six months before this incident, on the festival of *Teej.*

Among singers who were skilled in rhyming questions and answers in verse form in *kajli* competitions, Dulari was fantastically talented. She could put the most famous *kajli* singers to shame, and whoever had to compete against her was frightened. So, by having her on their side, the residents of Khojwa felt assured of their victory.

After the simple opening songs had stopped, the drum called forth a 16-year-old boy who stood up for the opposition. Pointing at Dulari, who was standing at the head of a group of women singers, he issued a challenge: "Hey, *Rani,* take this *promissory note!*" The people of Khojwa suddenly had doubts about their victory. The boy, Tunnu, was singing enthusiastically.

"Rani, take this promissory note. Take the special *ghevar* and *laddhu* made of molasses. And then, after putting a *tikka* dot on your forehead, Tuck the golden colored ribbon in your sari."

The *shanai* players repeated Tunnu's song on their instruments. The spectators were amazed. Contrary to her usual practice of responding in competition to the slightest provocation, Dulari hesitated to duel with the opposition and simply stayed quiet, keeping a smile on her face. Tunnu was challenging Dulari with his honeyed voice, and Dulari seemed infatuated by it.

This was Tunnu's third or fourth public performance. His father sat on the ghat all day, a priest for a handful of client families who lived in a poor part of town. In this capacity, he performed all sorts of religious activities, from the *satyanarayan* ceremony, to weddings and death rituals, struggling to provide for his household.

While his father toiled, Tunnu became addicted to poetry in the company of loafers. He made the great poet *Bhairohela* his *guru,* and then started composing beautiful kajlis. He was also

skilled in the poetic exchange of the singing competition; and on
the strength of this special talent, he was summoned by the people
of the Bajardiha neighborhood to represent them in that evening's
competition. When they heard his poetry, the people of Bajardiha
shouted, "Bravo, bravo!" but the faces of the Khojwa people had
blanched. While pointing to the dark, ripe, plumb-colored
complexion of Dulari, Tunnu said in poetic language:

"Why do people call you a woman, when you are really a
nightingale? Your color is like that of a nightingale, but your
voice even is sweeter than the coo of a nightingale. The female
crow raises the nightingale, and you too must have been raised by
someone else. The nightingale's eyes are red, and here also there
is a similarity as your eyes are gradually becoming red listening to
my song."

But Tunnu had made a mistake. Dulari's eyes were turning
red not from anger, but from the fire of *ganja*. When she heard his
charge, she broke out laughing, and Tunnu's song came to an end.

Then the beating of the drum started again, signaling a new
round. The sweet sound of the shanai echoed. Now, it was
Dulari's turn. She looked straight at Tunnu's fair, thin face with
her intoxicated eyes; and from her throat came a stream of
gurgling sounds:

"Oh, look at this, you talk to me this way! I'll scratch your
pale, leprous face. Your father spent his life looking after the
ghats, and scraping together small change, he's got a few paisa.
And you, good for nothing, have you ever seen money in your
life?"

Now the color had returned to the faces of the people of
Khojwa, and they started to shout, "Hurrah, hurrah!" Dulari was
singing:

"People, for no good reason, consider you to be a human, but
in reality you are a 'stork.' Your complexion is the white of a
stork's wing, and like the stork, you too are deceitful. Sooner or

128

later, a *fish bone* will get stuck in your throat and on that day your cover will disappear."

In response, Tunnu sang:

"You can abuse me to your heart's content, and in that way you can quench all the fire of your   passion, but I will continue to tell you the pain of my heart at the beat of a drum. Oh, Rani...."

When he heard this, Dulari's master, Fenku Sardar, grabbed hold of his stick and ran forward to beat Tunnu; but Dulari stepped in to protect him.

This was their first meeting. Even though many of those present wanted to hear more, neither continued to sing on that day. The atmosphere had turned unpleasant.

(3)

After sending Tunnu off, Dulari started to get hold of herself. Suddenly she realized that Tunnu was dressed completely differently today. She could see him in her mind's eye wearing a kurta of hand-spun cotton and a Gandhi cap, instead of his usual imported cloth kurta and his stylish Lucknow cap. She wanted to ask him why he was dressed this way, but there was no opportunity. Walking pensively over to her clothes chest, she opened it, and with great care, placed the sari given her by Tunnu under all the other clothes.

Her heart had become somewhat unsteady today. In their first meeting, she had already experienced Tunnu's weakness for her. But then she had thought it merely a temporary infatuation. Tunnu came to her house several times afterward, but never ventured a conversation. He would come in and, for half an hour or so, sit near Dulari. Even when Dulari asked him what he wanted, he wouldn't say anything. He'd just listen attentively to Dulari's conversation, and then slowly, like a shadow, sneak away.

Her youth on the brink of decline, Dulari would laugh to herself over Tunnu's infatuation. But today she felt compassion for the pale-complexioned, immature, lean boy. After 25 years of wandering through the dark valleys of her deprived world, Dulari was not slow in understanding that Tunnu was not attracted to her physically. No, what attracted him was related to her soul, not to her body. She also realized today that until now so much of the indifference she had shown had been artificial. The truth was that, in some secret corner of her heart there was a strong place for Tunnu. Still, she was not ready to admit this reality; she did not want to confront this truth. She was disturbed, and her confused mind started to look for something else to divert itself.

She lit the stove and busied herself in the kitchen. Just then, Fenku Sardar came into the room carrying a bundle of saris. When Dulari saw the bundle, she looked away. Fenku put it by her feet and said, "Look, what fine saris!"

"You promised to give me a sari on Holi," Dulari said, kicking the bundle.

"I'll fulfill that promise by Teej. Business is slow these days," Fenku countered.

"I heard that greedy people always profit from gambling," Dulari said.

"What do you know about the give and take of business? I have to pay the chief of police fifty rupees a day, and local police ten or twenty. By Teej, I'll be able to give you a Banaras sari for sure," Fenku said, assuring Dulari.

Dulari was about to answer Fenku when the country's revolutionary groups, just then collecting foreign clothing to burn, were making every room in the narrow Bhairavnath lane echo with their song, "Mother India, Hail To Thee."

On the street outside, four men had spread out a sheet and were holding onto the four corners. *Dhotis, saris, kurtas,* and hats were raining down onto it.

Suddenly Dulari opened her window and threw out Fenku's velvet cornered saris, newly woven with fine cotton made in the mills of Manchester and Lancashire. The eyes of the four men holding onto the cloth rose simultaneously in the direction of the window, because until then the majority of the clothes they had collected were torn and old. But, the new bundle had saris that hadn't even been unfolded yet. The eyes of all those in the procession along with those of the four cloth holders stared at the window hoping to find out who the thrower was, but just then the window slammed shut. The procession moved forward.

The person at the end of the procession, the secret police officer, Ali Sageer, also took in what had happened. He stroked his long moustache as his alert eyes noted the house number. Just then, one shutter of the window opened again, then closed with a slam. Ali Sageer took note that Dulari had opened the shutter, and that a man pushed her from the window with one hand, and with a jerk of the other hand closed the shutter. Catching a glimpse of the police informer, Fenku Sardar, the police officer's face registered the thin line of a smile. He moved a little forward, and, throwing a few *paise* in front of Benni, the pan vendor sitting on a platform, he ordered some pan.

(4)

Repeatedly beating the broad and strong back of Fenku Sardar with a broom while descending the stairs and making a loud thumping noise, Dulari shouted, "Get out, get out, and if you ever cross this threshold again, I'll bite your nose off."

In her rage, the upper end of Dulari's sari fell open. With nostrils inflamed, underlip throbbing, and eyes spitting out fire, her carefully tied bun of hair scattered all over her bare breasts, covering them modestly. As soon as Fenku had left the lane, she shut the door.

131

Once outside, he found himself face-to-face with the police inspector and, in spite of Fenku's embarrassment at his apparent helplessness, he found himself approaching Sageer after their eyes had made contact.

Back at her house, Dulari returned to her courtyard very slowly. Women friends and neighbors looked on curiously, but Dulari didn't even glance at them. After climbing the stairs, she entered her room and threw the broom against the door. *Dal* was simmering on the stove. With a kick, she overturned the pot, extinguishing the fire.

But the heart of Dulari kept on burning like a kiln. The neighbors came into the room and started to utter a stream of sweet words to extinguish their friend's blaze. Dulari's emotions started to cool down when one of Fenku's previous women, Bitto, blurted out, "Dulari, how dare you act like that to a man, especially one who keeps you like a queen?"

Dulari boiled up again. Looking at her well-exercised arms she said arrogantly, "If he keeps me like a queen, what sort of prize has he conquered? Didn't I hand over my invaluable honor? Isn't being deprived of the honor of a woman also a great sacrifice?"

Seeing Dulari flare up again, Kundan said, "You're right, sister dear. A body can be bought with money, not the spirit. But what really happened today?"

"It was jealousy, what else?" Dulari said, interrupting Kundan. "Tell me, did any of you ever see Tunnu coming here?"

"I can swear standing in the middle of the Ganges that Tunnu has never come here," the mother of Jhingur said, She completely forgot that she had seen Tunnu leaving Dulari's room just two hours before. The other women smiled at this, but no one contradicted her. Dulari again calmed down. Just then the nine-year-old Jhingur, with a fishing net thrown over his back, came into the courtyard and quickly relayed the news that white soldiers had shot Tunnu and that they had removed his body.

132

If this had been some other day, Dulari would have laughed and hurled some abuse at Tunnu's name. But today, when she heard the news, she was stunned. She didn't even ask where and under what circumstances the incident had taken place. The one whose heart had never before been moved suddenly became weak; and in her eyes, which had previously always burned with the harshness of a desert, dark clouds suddenly formed.

She made no attempt to hide the tears from her neighbors. They were astonished to see this softness in the quarrelsome, cold-hearted Dulari. Most of the them were fallen women, and the first sign of a truly fallen woman is that she is heartless. So they considered Dulari's reaction normal for an accomplished prostitute. Bitto even joked, "Those of us who are in this profession must not show any sadness at the loss of a dear one."

"I hate hiding things," Dulari said. "Whatever I've done, I've done openly." She stood up and, in front of everyone, opened the box and took out the hand-spun cotton sari stained with Tunnu's dark tears. She put the sari on, summoned Jhingur and asked him, "Where was Tunnu killed?"

Jhingur answered, "Town hall."

After she had left in the direction of the town hall, Fenku Sardar and a police secretary came in through the door; and Fenku said that Dulari would have to go to the police station to sing in a celebration convened by an *Aman Sabha.*

(5)

The chief news reporter threw down the copy of the story on his co-worker's desk and scolded him, "Sharmaji, it would be better if you opened a tea stall instead of being a reporter for this newspaper."

Sharmaji, frightened, squinted his confused eyes in an attempt to focus without his glasses, which he was then wiping on his *kurta,* and asked, "What? What's the matter?"

133

The chief reporter, irritated, asked, "That fantastic love story you've written page after page of—have you given any thought about where it would be printed and who would print it? Besides you, were there any other witnesses? If I were to print what you wrote today, this newspaper would be closed by tomorrow. The editor would end up in jail."

The editor's ears perked up on hearing something about himself. He asked, "What happened?"

"Oh, just this—an article by Sharmaji. I don't know why I'm beating my head against the wall," the chief reporter said.

"Read it," the editor ordered. The chief reporter handed over the article to Sharmaji and said, "Take it. You can try to explain it. Start with the title you put on it. What's the title?"

"Alas, this is 'Where My Nose Ring Got Lost,'" Sharmaji said, blushing. Then, very slowly, he started to read.

"Yesterday, the 6th of April, a total strike was observed following the appeal of the nationalist leaders that even precluded street vendors from making their rounds. Processions started in the early morning, and foreign clothes were being collected for burning. Participating in one of the processions was Tunnu, one of the city's well-known *kajli* singers. When this particular procession reached the town hall, it dispersed and the head of the constables, Ali Sageer, grabbed Tunnu and cursed him. When Tunnu objected, the chief of the constables kicked him, landing his boot in Tunnu's ribs, knocking him to the ground. A trickle of blood came out of his mouth. They lifted Tunnu up, loaded him into a white soldier's vehicle parked nearby and told the people they were going to take him to the hospital. But our reporter followed the car and learned that, in reality, Tunnu died. Our reporter witnessed Tunnu's body being lowered into the Varuna river at eight that night.

"In connection with this, it is worth noting the singer, Dulari, had a relationship with Tunnu. Yesterday, right at the celebration convened by the Aman Sabha—in which, indeed, not one

134

representative of the public was present—Dulari was made to dance and sing. She had perhaps already heard the news of Tunnu's death. She was very sad and wore only a simple, hand-spun cotton sari. It was said she was forcefully brought there by the police, and that she did not want to sing where, eight hours before, her lover was murdered. But, helpless, she stood up to sing. The infamous police constable, Ali Sageer, ordered her to sing some seasonal songs. Dulari laughed emptily and started singing with a painfully moving voice:

'Right here my nose ring got lost, oh Ram! Whom can I ask about it?'

"In the midst of this delightful atmosphere of fragrant flowers from the *Company Garden* a silence spread, pierced only by Dulari's echoing melody:

'Right here, alas, my nose ring got lost. Whom can I ask about it?'

"Fixing her sight on the place where Tunnu had been kicked and had fallen that afternoon, Dulari repeated, 'Right here, alas, my nose ring got lost,' and then looking with a questioning expression all around her she sang: 'Whom can I ask?' There was the faint line of a smile on her lip. She sang the next stanza of her song:

'Should I ask my mother-in-law? Should I ask my sister-in-law?

If I ask my brother-in-law I will feel so embarrassed.'

"Repeating this line about asking her brother-in-law, she turned around and levelled a look right at the police officer, Ali Sageer. Drops of tears showered from her eyes, or it might be said that some drops of the water that was splashed up by throwing Tunnu's body in the Varuna were now being manifest in the eyes of Dulari. Such a sight was never seen before—not during a dust storm, nor in the ocean, nor even when someone dies."

"That's the truth," the editor said, "but we can't print it."

135

Holi—a major Hindu festival in which people throw colored water and powders at each other to herald the advent of Spring. It ends in friends and relatives gathering to share food or 'bhang,' (opium) in sweets or sherbets. A month or two before the festival, men gather to sing songs related to the festival, the season, and to love.

Kajal—a black paste Indian men and women put around their eyes for decoration and for good health.

Teej—a festival when married women often return temporarily to their parents' home, having spent the time since their marriage with their husband's family. Singing kajlis is a popular activity at this time of year.

Kajli—a type of folk song.

Rani—a queen.

Promissory note—a sign of affection as used in this context.

Ghevar and laddu—two popular types of sweets.

Tikka dot—a dot of color, daubed ritually in the middle of the forehead.

Shanai—a type of flute.

Satyanarayan ceremony—a ritual in which Vishnu is worshipped, usually carried out on the occasion of some anticipated or realized good fortune such as a wedding or job promotion.

Bhairohela—a legendary folk artist of Banaras.

Guru—a teacher or spiritual guide, and in Banaras, a widely used term of respect.

Nightingale—refers to folk beliefs about nightingales and crows. The nightingale is believed to be raised by the crow, a reference probably to Dulari's dubious parentage. Also comparing Dulari to the nightingale, renowned for its sweet voice, is a compliment. However, the bird is also black and for a woman a dark complexion is not considered attractive.

Ganja—an intoxicant from the hemp plant.

Fish bone—emphasizing the idea of deceit, Dulari paints a picture of a Brahmin who eats fish but whose pious father, we can assume, is a strict vegetarian.

136

"Mother India, Hail To Thee"—from a song, "Bande Mataram" by Bankim Chandra Chatterjee, which was the anthem of the freedom movement. The song identifies India with the mother earth goddess.

Aman sabha—a citizen group formed by prominent people whenever communal tensions increase in the city. In the period of the story, such groups probably included police collaborators acting against the independence movement.

Ji—an honorific suffix.

Company Garden—a city park located opposite the town hall, named for the British East India Company.

POSTSCRIPT

Folk Music in Banaras

An important part of this story's background is Banaras' rich and varied tradition of folk music. For example, here the author has used a *kajli* singing competition as the background for the romance between his two main characters, and he has taken the title of this story from a *chaiti,* another type of song. Similarly, the previous story starts at a *lavni* type of singing competition, and most of the story titles of this collection have come from folk songs. By his frequent use of folk music, Shiv Prasad Mishra has emphasized an important part of Banaras' popular culture— one often obscured by the city's central place in India's classical music tradition.[1] Also, because many of these musical forms have disappeared or diminished in popularity in recent years as film music and loudspeakers take over previous forms of popular musical entertainment, the author may have been attempting to capture a musical past of Banaras of which he was obviously personally very fond.

In addition to musical qualities such as melody, the different types of Banaras folk music can be described by both their content and the context in which they are performed. For example, in content, *kajlis* are usually love songs, like the one in this story; while the *lavni* of the previous chapter is typically a song about heroes and martyrs. In context, both *kajlis* and *lavnis* may be sung in competitions between groups or individuals representing *muhallas* (neighborhoods) or *akharas,* (clubs). However, whereas a lavni competition may focus more on the quality of singing, improvisational kajlis are more a contest of impromptu creativity, with one side offering a theme and the other side developing it and offering it back to the first for further development. Context is also associated with season: a kajli competition is likely to take place in the

---

[1] For more on the popular nature of folk music in Banaras, see Nita Kumar, *The Artisans of Banaras,* Princeton University Press, Princeton, NJ, 1988, Chapter 6, pp. 125-154, and Scott Marcus, "The Rise of a Folk Music Genre: Biraha," in Sandria B. Freitag, ed., *Culture and Power in Banaras,* University of California Press, 1988, pp. 93-113.

rainy season—believed to be a soft and sensuous time of year when the earth is lush and green—while a lavni is more often a springtime event.

In addition to distinguishing music types by content and context, some folksongs are associated with rites of passage, such as birth or marriage, whereas others are related to festivals. The festival of Holi, mentioned in this story, is an occasion for several different kinds of songs. The festival itself is held at the beginning of Chait and celebrates the mythological victory of good over evil as portrayed in the tale of Hiranyakasipu.[1] The celebration starts with hundreds of bonfires set around the city, continues with participants throwing colored water at one another, and ends with friends and family getting together and sharing food or bhang. For a month or two before the festival, men gather to sing many different types of songs related to the season, to the festival, and to love.

---

[1] King Hiranyakasipu, in his excessive vanity, ordered all his subjects to worship him, rather than the gods. His son, Prahalada, was a devotee of Vishnu, and so refused to obey his father's order. Angered by his son's impudence, Hiranyakasipu tried to have him killed on several occasions. At one point, the king had his sister, Holika, carry Prahalada on her lap into a bonfire. Because she possessed the power of immunity to fire, both Holika and the king thought that Prahalada would perish while she survived. The result, however, was the opposite: Holika burned to ashes and Prahalada left the fire unscathed. Hiranyakasipu was eventually killed by Vishnu in his half-man, half-lion incarnation, and his oppressed subjects celebrated wildly.

139

Figure 8.—A view of the Adi Keshav Temple at Adi Keshav Ghat which is mentioned in the following story. This scene was painted by William Daniell and published in an 1835 edition of the *Oriental Annual or Scenes of India*. Immediately below the temple is the confluence of the Ganges and Varuna Rivers. The sparsely inhabited central area of Banaras in the 1830s can be seen in the background of the sketch.

10

This Mortal Body for Ram

Introduction

*In addition to continuing the previous tale of the prostitute Dulari,
this story describes a protest that took place in 1891 that was known as
"Ram Halla" or "The Tumult of Ram." The incident, which began with
British plans to construct a water-pumping station on the shore of the
Ganges, is often held up as a symbol of the potential unity of Muslims
and Hindus in Banaras.*

*The incident occurred because the site chosen for the pumping
station was adjacent to a Hindu temple referred to as "Sitaram," and
this proximity alarmed a number of citizens. At first, their concern
centered on the engineer's entering the temple wearing his shoes, a sign
of disrespect.*

*However, with the digging of a deep ditch around the temple,
effectively preventing entrance, the citizens of Banaras started to take
direct action. First, a group of prominent citizens wrote a letter of protest
which the authorities ignored. Then, taking matters into their own hands,
a party of protestors filled in the ditch with stones and sand. Shortly
afterward, a rumor spread that the British intended to destroy the temple.
In response, on the seventh day of the Hindu month of Chait, two days
before the traditional celebration of the birth of Ram (the "Ramnomi"
referred to in the story), the protesters declared a general strike closing
markets and shops. That evening they held a public meeting at the town
hall, and a crowd of about 4,000 people—Muslims as well as Hindus—
went to the site of the temple at Bhadeini, near Assi. As they proceeded,
the crowd chanted, "Ram-Kaj Chanabhangu Sarira" or "This mortal
body for Ram," a phrase taken from the work of Tulsi Das and the title of
this story. They surrounded the site and threw the pump machinery into
the Ganges. The crowd then went on a rampage, destroying street lamps,*

the telegraph office, and other public facilities. In the end, in spite of some citizens of Banaras receiving prison sentences for their part in the incident, the temple remained standing and, indeed, can be visited today.[1]

Some attribute the nineteenth-century unity of the Hindu and Muslim communities in Banaras to the efforts of the elites of the city, especially the Maharajah, while others say the unity of this period is due to the underlying cultural similarity that exists between the two communities despite their vastly different religious beliefs. While, indeed, it does appear that the two groups have cooperated and shown considerable evidence of mutual tolerance in the past—perhaps more than in other north Indian cities—these days neither conflict between them nor the authorities' imposition of an occasional curfew to quell communal tensions is unusual.

In the opening paragraph three Sita-Rams are mentioned. The first is the temple, the principal figures of worship in which are Sita and Ram. The second is the head priest, a mahant *named Sitaram. The third is a* rais, *a wealthy property holder, also named Sitaram.*

Words and phrases in italics are explained in a glossary at the end of the story. Also, a postscript to this story, found after the glossary, contains notes on Muslims in Banaras and on the digestive, pan.

(1)

The temple of Sitaram was destroyed. The Mahant Sitaram raised an outcry, and the *rais,* Sitaram, has been ruined."

While Beni *Tamoli,* a peddler of *paan,* was busy filtering the lime paste that he had mixed with curd, this phrase kept echoing in his mind. Last night was the first time he met the beggar-woman of the ruins, but she had a strong effect on him He

---

[1] Details of this event are described in Thakur Prasad Singh, *Svatantrata-Andolan aur Banaras*, Vishvavidyalay Prakashan, Banaras, 1990, pp. 36-7, and Sandria B. Freitag, "State and Community: Symbolic Popular Protest in Banaras's Public Arenas," in Sandria B. Freitag, ed., *Culture and Power in Banaras*, University of California Press, Berkeley, 1989, pp.203-28.

found her words extremely soothing, and kept thinking how right she was that the fire of the mind stills when the heart is alight with love.

Meanwhile, the lime mixture was ready. He arranged the little earthen pots of catechu, lime, and betel nut in his basket of *paan*. He then set it on his waist and walked out of his house. As was his custom, he came to the steps in front of Dulari's house, but he immediately saw that police had taken over the place. A large, surging crowd had gathered in this narrow lane. The faces of the people were full of curiosity and fear, while those of police glowed with a fake seriousness.

Beni stood against the wall to one side and looked for something that might tell him why the crowd had come. He knew about Dulari's bad reputation. He also believed that, in general, people were always curious to see well-known men and women of ill repute. So there was nothing that struck him as particularly unusual in a crowd of people milling around Dulari's house. But why the police?

Answers to this question were as plentiful as the mouths of people watching. But the most important fact he could deduce was that Dulari had hanged herself by a sari. Her corpse was still hanging there from a rafter. It was a suicide; no doubt about it. The only question was why Dulari killed herself; and Beni was the only one who had the answer. But after taking in what was happening, he just put his basket of *paan* under his arm and left the crowd.

At the water fountain where the lane turns, some women had gathered to get water. Among them was Jhingur, a boy of about ten, talking like a politician. The women were entertained by the high-sounding oration of the boy.

The reason Jhingur was getting such attention was that he and his mother rented the room under the place where Dulari killed herself. If a man has a famous head on his shoulders, even the dust on his feet is respected; and so, too, Beni thought, the

143

unworthy sometimes receive respect simply because of close contact with the worthy. Jhingur was talking like an adult, "I know all about why this prostitute killed herself. Because of the affair with Tunnu, her relationship with Fenku turned bad, and she was worried about who would take care of her when she got old, so she killed herself."

While women are amused by such adult talk like this from so immature a mouth, men get annoyed. The young women, biting the end of their saris, started to laugh, and the old women, attempting to smile sincerely, made their toothless faces even more deformed, and said only, "What you say is true." But the men standing nearby were not charmed. "Get out of here," a few chided him. "Mind your own business."

Beni heard what Jhingur was saying, turned in disgust, and walked away. His feet took him in the direction of the ruined fort of Raj Ghat.

He found himself at the bend in the road to Raj Ghat at Machodari. Right there, Beni saw the platform, and he felt sad. Only twelve hours before, while returning from the ruined fort, a tired Dulari had sat down on that very platform to rest for ten minutes. And now she had gone so far away that even a thought, if it tried to reach her, would get tired. In spite of his sorrow, Beni smiled at the transitory nature of the human mind and body. Then he moved on. He kept thinking how strange the previous evening had been.

That evening he set off to the Ganges to ask the river's rolling waves, "Hey, tell me, where have you hidden my new bride?" Reaching Adi Keshav Ghat, he thought that to find her, he would have to jump in and question Mother Ganges herself. Just as he was climbing up the steps of the ghat onto a pedestal to jump, he saw Dulari sitting on the last step of the ghat, trying to tie her arms and legs with her sari. Hesitating, he noticed that Dulari had rolled herself into the water. Beni leapt off the

144

pedestal, and when he reemerged from the river he was pulling Dulari by her braid.

He laid her down on the step, and then sat a little distance from her. Immediately after her rescue Dulari complained, "Hey, betel-nut man, why did you pull me out?"

"Oh, Dulari, I didn't do anything wrong. My own wife drowned and disappeared," Beni answered. "It's very painful to drown."

"You didn't do me any favor saving me," Dulari said bitterly. "My heart is on fire. Drowning would have extinguished the flame."

Beni was going to respond when someone from above said, "This fire will not be put out by water, but rather the fire of the mind stills when the heart is alight with love."

Dulari and Beni together raised their eyes and saw a middle-aged woman, in dirty dress, standing about four steps above them. She looked about 55, with some life still in her beauty. In spite of her age, her face had few lines on it. Perhaps her own fire had been quick and intense so there was little smoke. The two kept staring at this stranger. She spoke again: "It's a winter evening. You shouldn't stay wet. Come with me."

Her voice echoed with authority; Beni and Dulari could not disobey her. They followed her to an underground room in the unused part of the old ruined fort. The room was quite large. In one corner was a grave. Although it was a simple grave of clay, it had recently been whitewashed. Flowers were scattered around it. At the head of the grave was a flickering clay lamp. Beni and Dulari took in the scene, standing still. The stranger removed a sari from a bag that was hanging on a wall peg, and handing it over to Dulari, she said to both, "What are you looking at? This is the tomb of a brave man who considered love to be a God for whom he gave his life."

Dulari and Beni lowered their heads naturally in respect for the grave in front of them.

145

As he was walking along, the scenes of the previous night in the underground room were passing through Beni's mind. He was thinking about how educated the old beggar woman of the ruins was. Whatever she said, she said in poetic form. After Dulari had changed her sari, she asked them a question in poetic form:

"Why have you become so indifferent to life?

Why are you so ready to drown?"

If Beni had been a poet or if he had been educated, he might have answered her this way:

"Since death one day is certain,

Why am I not able to sleep all night?"

And if the intellectual level of Dulari had been a little higher, and she also possessed the ability to answer poetically like this unknown woman, then probably she would have responded:

"Without you, my lover, I am still alive,

But I cannot believe how I have managed."

Since neither of them was capable of this, Beni was only able to say, "The waves of the Ganges stole the garden of my life." Dulari just took a deep breath and remained silent.

At this the woman again asked, "After losing your lovers, don't you have some keepsake to love in their place? Perhaps by looking at it, you'll be able to live."

In response, Beni said, "In searching for my drowned wife, I came upon a cow."

Dulari said, "Before he died, my lover gave me a sari of handwoven cotton."

As soon as she heard this, the woman responded bitterly, "Then the two of you are great cowards. Why aren't you able to live when you have these precious things?"

"It's very difficult to live with such sorrow," Dulari responded quietly, hesitantly, her face lowered.

"Wrong, you're completely wrong," the woman shot back. "In this world the easiest thing to do is die sadly, even in happiness, and the hardest thing is to lead a life happily in sadness."

Dulari started to laugh. "That's just a saying," she said. "Who can really live happily in sadness?"

The woman replied as if she were burned, "You won't have to go far to see such a person. Just look at me. You want to hear how happy I am? To whom does this room belong if not me? Whenever I want, I go anywhere I want. There is no one here to stop me. I sleep when I want, and I get up when I want. No one is here to interrupt me. In the morning, I put a veil over my face, take a bowl in my hand, and go out to beg. Whatever I get, I eat happily. And I can take pleasure in the memory of my friend when I spread out my bedding next to this tomb. If you want to hear about my sadness, then listen to my tragic story. Do you want to hear it?"

Beni and Dulari urged her to go on.

The old woman started like this:

"This story is like a dream; that I had when I was young.

"The temple of Sitaram was demolished. Mahant Sitaram raised an outcry. The *rais* Sitaram was ruined. For two days it was like an earthquake in Banaras. So many promising young men were turned to dust. For 48 hours there was such an inferno that my love garden was burned. The flower of my dreams turned to ashes. This curse—this accident—this historical event is called Ram Halla in Banaras."

Beni and Dulari were familiar with the words "Ram Halla," but they had never known the whole story, which was deeply inscribed in the memory of the previous generation of Banarasis. Their curiosity grew, and the woman kept on speaking.

"My father, Shah Ataullah, used to take care of the tomb of a Muslim saint. My mother was a Hindu, who for some reason, was excommunicated from her caste and became a Muslim. Father

147

gave me the name, "Star of the Sky." Mother used to call me simply "Star." But as soon as I became older, I considered myself the moon of the land. I was born in the month of Chait. In that month I was married and in that same month I became a widow. My mother used to say that in Chait, Ram himself was born."

Looking directly into the past as if piercing the curtain of time, the old beggar kept on talking, "Yes, it is in the month of Chait and I am 15 years old and I have just married. My husband, Shah Shahabudin, is such an attractive young man that whoever looks at him just keeps on looking. Yesterday was the first day of my wedding. In the room, the moonlike one who had just become a wife is seated near her sunlike husband. From the street, someone is shouting. A beautiful young man with a splendid full beard comes running, saying that the Hindus and Muslims of Banaras should know that in Assi, the ancient temple of Sitaram is being destroyed to make way for the construction of a water tank. 'Today a temple is being destroyed. Tomorrow it will be a mosque. Come out and save it, save it'."

The woman took a deep breath, "When we heard the compelling voice of the man who, I later came to know, was named Mahant Sitaram, our hearts were wrung with anguish. Mother came running and said, 'Son, look what is happening.' My husband, whom I had affectionately started to call "the king of young beauty," immediately left. My mother started to talk to me, 'My star, this situation is very grave. Ram is also a name of God. To tell you the truth, all love and affection are God.'

"Hearing what my mother was saying, father laughed and said in her support, *'Majnun sees Allah in the form of Layla!'* My beautiful husband had returned from the lane, and standing on the threshold, was overhearing what we were saying. He only asked, 'Mother, do I have your permission to go?' My mother and father immediately said, 'Yes, this is the work of God.' Then the two of them left us alone in the room. My husband came inside and asked also for my permission. When I heard this, I was stunned. I

148

gathered up my courage and asked, 'What will happen to me?' My husband took the garland of roses from his neck and placed it around mine. Then he went away."

The eyes of the woman filled with tears. She took a deep breath and spoke again. "Then what happened? The Hindus and Muslims of Banaras went to Assi Ghat and threw the large machines that were to be used in the water-works into the Ganges as if they were playballs. After this the looting started. People believed that the hand of a *rais* named Sitaram was behind the temple's destruction. A crowd is just like sheep; they all went to attack Sitaram's house. My husband said, 'We won't cooperate in this looting.' As he was about to leave with all the other Muslims, God only knows who fired a bullet. That bullet hit my husband. The crowd scattered, but he somehow managed to reach the shore of the Ganges, and there he collapsed. On that night—without saying anything to my mother and father—I went out in search of him. Finding him unconscious on the river shore, I somehow got him into a boat and brought him to this room. Oh, how much I tried to save him, but that very night he died. It was the night of Ramnomi. Staying awake the whole night, I made a grave for him. Look."

Beni and Dulari looked at the grave. "Not that," the woman laughed. "Look at this." And she held up a locket tied around her neck by a string. She opened it. In it were little fragments of dry flowers. The woman took out a thin string which once held the flowers. Showing it to Dulari, she said, "Look, with the help of this thread I have spent my sad life happily—and you have an entire sari."

As he walked along, Beni thought to himself, "What use Dulari made of the sari in hanging herself!"

149

GLOSSARY

Tamoli—a caste name for those who make paan.

Paan—a mixture of betel nut, lime, and other ingredients wrapped in a betel leaf and chewed.

Adi Keshav Ghat—Banaras' northernmost ghat, i.e., stairs descending to the river, located at the confluence of the Varuna and Ganges Rivers. Today, a temple to Lord Vishnu stands in this prominent place, where Vishnu (Keshav) is said to have once washed his holy feet.

Excommunicated from her caste—this may have occurred because the beggar's mother had violated an important caste norm—for example, engaging in a relationship with a Muslim or someone of a different caste—and so to uphold the honor of the caste her identity as a caste member was removed.

Chait—a month in the Hindu calendar that falls during March- April.

"Majnun sees Allah in the form of Layla!"—a reference to an ancient Persian love story in which Majnun and Layla fell deeply in love, but Layla's family prevented their marriage. Majnun's insanity over his loss took on mystical/spiritual overtones in which Allah and his former lover, Layla, became one.

150

POSTSCRIPT

Muslims in Banaras

In this center of Hinduism, the place of the Muslim population seldom receives much attention despite its long history, size, and economic significance. Muslims first took up residence in the city with the invasion of Muhammad Ghuri in the eleventh century. Since then, through conversion and immigration, Muslims have come to make up about a quarter of the city's population. Most Muslims in the city are handloom weavers or work as helpers in a weaver's family, and produce the renowned Banaras silk sari distributed throughout India and the world. (Ironically, the sari is almost exclusively worn by Hindu women.) In addition, the Muslim presence in Banaras is visible in a few, very prominent mosques, and the main Muslim market at Dal Mandi, notable for its butcher shops and the smell of grilled meat not found elsewhere in this mostly vegetarian city.

Another main feature of the Muslim presence are the *mazars* or tomb-shrines built to the martyrs who sacrificed their lives for Islam. The *mazars* are believed to be auspicious, sacred places where blessings may be requested and received, where special fairs, picnics, and outings are held, and where singing events are organized at night.[1]

Perhaps the author is trying to pay some respect to this often unrepresented section of Banaras' population by focusing on the "Ram Halla" incident and by situating part of the action of this story near a Muslim's tomb at the old fort on Raj Ghat, immediately north of the bridge over the Ganges, where some of the most famous mazars of the city are located. The importance of the diversity of Banaras' population is further underlined by the use of Raj Ghat as the scene of this story, since it is the site of many excavations that have contributed to an understanding of Banaras' Jain and Buddhist past as well as its Hindu roots.

---

[1] Nita Kumar, "The Mazars of Banaras: A New Perspective on the City's Sacred Geography," *The National Geographical Journal of India*, Vol. 33, pt. 3, September 1987, pp. 263-267.

Paan

Paan, like the sari, is made in other cities as well as in Banaras, and, like the sari, as any Banarasi will claim, it achieves its highest standard in their city. Literally, "paan" is a specially prepared leaf into which fragments of betel nut, lime and other pastes, spices, and tobacco are placed and folded together. The most distinguishing ingredient in this mix is catechu, a gum which comes from tree bark and is then prepared specially by the paan vendor according to his recipe. (Banarasi pan consumers claim that they can identify one pan from another based exclusively on the taste of catechu.)

The entire paan package goes into one's mouth, where, resting against the cheek, it dissolves into a thick, red saliva. Paan is sold throughout the city, mostly in little shops where men gather to discuss politics, local news, and gossip, usually with their heads tilted backwards to keep the red saliva from dripping onto and staining their clothing. Sometimes when the *tamoli,* or paan-vendor, does not have the capital to set up a shop, he will go from house to house selling his product, like the Beni Tamoli of this story. It is believed that paan can purify blood, rectify common health problems, restore normal breathing, and make bad breath smell good. Hence paan, to Banarasis, is more than a leaf and betel—it is a digestive, a catalyst for socializing, and one of the great joys of life.[1]

---

[1] Sushma Gupta, "Banaras ki Shan: Zarda va Paan," in *op. cit.*, pp. 111-4.

11

On This Side the Ganga,
On the Other the Yamuna

Introduction

The title of this story is a popular expression that originally comes from a song describing the difficulties of choosing between two compelling alternatives which is what the characters in this story must do. Both the Ganga (Ganges) and the Yamuna are sacred rivers and the names of both are employed, as in this story, for people and animals.

Words and phrases in italics are explained in a glossary at the end of the story. Also, a postscript to this story, found after the glossary, contains notes on caste in India.

Ganga was the name of an innocent young woman who refused to be flattered by the stares and sighs of her neighbors' longings. But to those neighbors, from the highest—the sahib, Rai Sadhuram—down to all the servants of the neighborhood, including even the laborer, Sidhua Kahar, an unexpected glimpse of her beauty was a blessing. If on the one hand, Rai Sahib was ready to make her the head of the women's works in his factory, then on the other, Sidhua wanted to make her the queen of his heart and worship her. Old and young—boys about to be young men, middle-aged men about to say good-bye to their youth—all were interested in taking a dip in their Ganga. They saw in her eyes an intoxicating mixture of foreign wine and country-distilled liquor. Those who drank from fancy cups, as well as those who sipped from crude clay cups, wanted to savor every sip of Ganga that they could imagine.

In the mornings and evenings when Ganga, dressed in a black sari, went out of her house with her clay pitcher fixed on her hip, the good fortune of the amorous poets appeared to have awakened. When they started to recite their poetry, Ganga would laugh at the youthfulness of the old men, frown on the childishness of the young men, and go on her way. To the onlookers, there was a special flavor even in Ganga's irritation.

Ganga was the daughter of an *ahir*. Without a brother and father, and abandoned by her husband, she lived with her mother. How many times had her mother urged Ganga to remarry. Still all of her mother's anger couldn't change a simple "no" from Ganga into a "yes." So, when the subject of marriage came up, mother and daughter usually argued.

One day just after getting up, this dynamic had gotten underway. Ganga was about to sweep out the courtyard, and her mother was about to churn buttermilk. Both were absorbed in their work, when suddenly Ganga's mother shouted out, "Ganga!"

Ganga didn't answer. She was searching for some ray of light in the thick darkness of her mind. Her mother called out again, "Ganga!" Ganga ignored her again. While her broom was chasing away the dust, a ray of light in her mind was also flying away. Then Ganga's mother lost her patience. She yelled, "Ganga, are you deaf? Why don't you answer?"

Suppressing her sadness, Ganga answered, surprised, "Did you call me mother?"

"If it wasn't me, what husband is sitting here who might have called you?"

Ganga raised her sad eyes as if to ask her mother: "Is this what you called me for?"

Ganga's mother snapped back, "What are you staring at? Take this milk and yogurt to Rai Sahib's. I don't feel good today."

Ganga hesitated and then answered softly, "I can't go there."

"Sure, you won't be able to go there. You, after all, are a queen. How could you do such a petty job? Yes, of course, if you were going around and flirting with everyone in the neighborhood, you'd get ready in no time."

"You're jabbering nonsense. For heaven's sake, don't you have just a little fear of God?"

"You threaten me with God! You bitch! You won't deliver the milk. You won't lift a finger around the house. And I don't have it in me to carry on the work of running a household any more. Who else is here to do your work? When I tell you, 'get married,' you turn hot as if you've got malaria. You don't come from such a high caste that getting remarried will ruin you."

"How many times have I told you, mother, that everyone has their own choices to make."

"So you want to have it your way! I tell you, you'll have to get married. If not, then at least work as a servant in Rai Sahib's house. I don't know how many times that great man has already spoken to me about this."

"Why are you shouting, 'Marry! Marry!' I won't get married and I won't go to work in Rai Sahib's house. Offer me any other place, and I'll take it."

"Do you think that there's a job waiting for you somewhere just for the asking! Ha, she's only the daughter of an *ahir,* and thinks she won't get remarried."

"So you're also an *ahir's* daughter. Why didn't you ...."

"What are you saying, you black-faced bitch!" As she said this, Ganga's mother threw the churner at Ganga, hitting her in the forehead. Both the tears from her eyes and blood from the cut started to flow. Ganga shook with pain and leapt up furiously. But then in the next moment, she checked herself, her vision overwhelmed by darkness.

(2)

Beni lived in a modest house in front of Ganga's house.

When the first rays of sunlight fell on Beni's face, he opened his eyes, rubbed them, and then, after *kissing his palms,* he stretched a little and got up.* As he stood, he looked at Ganga in her courtyard. He heard Ganga and her mother arguing, saw Ganga's misery and her mother's anger. Then Beni saw the blood on the Ganga's forehead and the tears in her eyes. Pity, hatred, anger, and perhaps a little stream of affection flowed through the middle of Beni's heart. He heard the old woman shouting and saying, "I've explained so much that my tongue is broken. So much stubbornness! You're not a child that needs this explained! And anyway, what's all this got to do with me! If I die today, tomorrow will be just another day. What I say is for your benefit. But who listens? Who understands? Your luck is burning up. I went to Rai Sahib just for you. I begged and I prayed with folded hands. God bless him, may he have a lot of children and be

---

* See glossary

156

prosperous. The good man immediately said, 'Ganga's mother, don't worry. Whenever you want, bring her to me. There's a family in this home, servants, and maids. If she lives here properly, she'll have a good life.'

Beni could see that Ganga didn't reply. She was quiet for a while. Then she got up, washed her forehead wound with water, and after lifting the pitcher, wiped her eyes and left. Beni's eyes followed Ganga.

Outside, in one small open room, a *Pundit* was chanting the *Gita*, "Oh, Brave One, there is no doubt, the mind is restless and difficult to control." Then a familiar sound possessed the Pundit's restless mind, and he saw Ganga in a red sari as if, under the glow of dawn, he was seeing the vanishing beauty of light. Out of his mouth came, "Hey, Arjuna," and to finish the sentence he said in Sanskrit, "There she is in the reddish dress of sunflowers." Ganga kept going, but the reading of the Gita was postponed for that day.

The 60-year-old scribe tucked a pen behind his ear and, putting an ink-stained portfolio under his arm, left his house. Just as he was crossing the threshold, his sight stubbed its toe against a rock of beauty: Ganga was coming towards him. The scribe beamed, and stopped, astonished. Now Ganga was closer. The scribe interrupted her, "Tell me Ganga, how are things? Have you heard any more? Rai Sahib is worried about your marriage. But we know you very well. I explained clearly to Rai Sahib, 'She's a girl from this neighborhood. She's good. If she doesn't want to get married, why do you worry?' If the people of the neighborhood will share their bread with you, you'll manage. And dear, as I've said before, I don't have any children, so if you come to me and take care of my household, everything will be yours after I go. If not, the government will take it. Isn't that right?"

Instead of answering, she only asked, "Grandpa, have you made the arrangements for your funeral shroud?"

157

The scribe was disheartened, but forcing a smile he said, "There's a line in a poem that goes, *'I wonder, tying a shroud around my head...'*"

Ganga didn't understand the line, but kept on her way. Beni, as if having made a telescope of his eyes, saw the scene and, as if with telephonic ears, heard everything. His eyes became teary and his earlobes turned red. Then a deep voice called up from the courtyard, "Ma!" Beni's attention was diverted, and he answered, "I'll be right there, Yamuna," and quickly ran down the stairs.

(3)

Yamuna was not a human, she was an animal—a creature with four legs, two horns, and a tail. With great affection, Hindus call this creature the "mother cow." Beni's family consisted of only two living beings—himself and Yamuna.

Beni was a *paan* seller and managed well, living in quarters over his shop. Since his birth, there had been only two residents in this house at any one time. At first, Beni's parents lived there but, just two hours after giving birth to Beni, his mother was taken to the other world. Then, Beni and his father lived in the house. Beni's father became both father and mother, nurturing Beni and raising him. Beni's marriage was arranged in the countryside, and his father led the wedding party happily to the bride's house. The wedding took place but, while the wedding party was returning, a snake bit Beni's father. In the delirium of the poison, Beni's father chose the road to the other world instead of the one to his home. So then, just Beni and his wife lived in the house.

Once, during the season of heavy rains. Beni and his wife went to the Ganges to bathe, but a torrential monsoon flood carried Beni's wife away. Boats went to rescue her. After frantically searching six or seven hours, Beni could not find her body, but he did find a cow floating in the flood.

158

He lost his wife and found a cow. From then on, Beni and his cow, Yamuna, lived together in the house. Beni treated his cow with devotion, and in this he found pleasure and enjoyment. In the hot weather, he would close his shop and untie the cow in the lane in front of his house. Then, sitting on the platform running along the outside of his shop and fanning Yamuna, he would sing out in a heart-rending voice, "Oh beloved, you left me and my hut is forlorn;" The neighbors would sleep soundly, but Beni's song would steal away the sleep of Ganga, who as much as she tried, could not fall asleep. The echo of Beni's song would resonate in Ganga's heart, "Oh beloved, you left me and my house is forlorn," and in this way, half the night would pass. Eventually, Beni would tie Yamuna in the courtyard and go to sleep. In the morning, he would wash her and only then bathe himself.

On that day too, hearing Yamuna's call, Beni ran downstairs. He untied her and went to the tap. Ganga was standing there. "Hey Ganga, are you all right?" Beni asked.

"The day is passing. What else?"

"That's right." Beni started rubbing Yamuna and washing her. Ganga said, "Beni, no one treats anyone as well as you treat that animal. Why do you do it?"

"What am I doing, Ganga? A person has to do something. If not, how could I survive? The loneliness would poison me."

They were both quiet. Ganga filled her pitcher. Yamuna and Beni bathed. The three returned together. Ganga looked affectionately at Yamuna, "Your cow's very pretty. Is that why you love her so?"

"Beauty is in the eye of the beholder, Ganga. What we like strikes us as pretty."

Ganga said softly, "You're right." They returned to their houses. It was evening now.

For Beni, the day was filled with restlessness and confusion, struggling over something he had been ignoring for some time.

159

He couldn't even bring himself to open his shop. On the one hand, there was Ganga and, on the other, Yamuna. Today all the vague memories that had started to fade away came to Beni again one after the other. His life from birth until now had been unfolding in front of him like in a movie. In his eye was Ganga, his hand on Yamuna's back, and from his mouth came, "Ganga."

Ganga opened the door and walked into Beni's house. She said, "What is it? How did you know that I was coming? Anyway, I have a question, aren't we poor considered to have any *dharma*?"

"We have, Ganga, but not in the body, rather in the heart. The *dharma* of the poor is in our hearts."

Ganga's eyes lit up and she said, "So, then, why have people become our enemies? Why do they want to take away our dharma?" Beni looked quizzically at Ganga, who went on, "Today I went to Rai Sahib's house to deliver milk. I didn't exactly go, rather I was forcibly sent. He started to tell me, 'Ganga, if you do not show compassion towards me, I'll become a *sadhu*. The business which I've built up will be ruined. My family will starve, and the sin for all of this will fall on your head.' At home my mother also says, 'If you do not serve in Rai Sahib's house, I'll kill myself.' That foolish woman doesn't know what kind of man Rai Sahib is! Tell me, what should I do?"

"Nothing, Ganga. Rai Sahib won't become a *sadhu*, and your mother won't kill herself."

"No, Beni, when Rai Sahib said that today, he took an oath."

"It's a lie. He'll never become a *sadhu*."

"And if he becomes one, then what?"

"Nothing will ever happen. Such people don't turn into holy men and renounce everything suddenly."

"What kind of people become *sadhus*?"

"What kind of people? Look, from now on, this house, all my money, and all the other things in this house, everything, is yours, and I'm going away with Yamuna. Those who should be *sadhus*, Ganga, they just do it. There's no need to talk about it."

With just a cloth over his shoulder and the tether to Yamuna in his hand, Beni walked out of the house. A stunned Ganga listened to Beni, who was singing with feeling:

"On this side Ganga, on the other Yamuna,
and in the middle, build a hut before you leave."

The first line of a song then came out of Ganga's mouth:
"How will the days be passed? Tell me what to do."

GLOSSARY
(in order of appearance in the text)

Ahir—a caste name for those who raise cows and buffalos and process and sell dairy products.

Kissing his palms—the oldest scriptures of Hinduism, the Vedas, direct that a Hindu, upon awakening, should look to his hands in order to behold an auspicious object as the first thing he sees in the morning.

Pundit—a title for a learned person, often a Brahmin.

Gita—This refers to the *Bhagavad Gita*, a part of the epic *Mahabharata* and considered to contain one of the most important teachings of Lord Krishna, revered by Hindus.

Arjuna—the central figure of the epic *Mahabharata* of which the *Bhagavad Gita* or *Gita* is a part.

'I wonder, tying a shroud around my head...'—a line from a well-known poem of the Indian independence movement intended to convey the fearlessness of the freedom fighters. Here it is supposed to imply that, like the freedom fighters, the scribe is not afraid of death.

Paan—a mixture of betel nut, lime, and other ingredients wrapped in a betel leaf and chewed.

Dharma—a reference to the code of conduct of one's caste, i.e., the proper behavior and moral conduct through the observance of caste rules which define an individual's responsibilities and obligations.

Sadhu—an ascetic, holy person who is supposed to have renounced all worldly possessions.

162

POSTSCRIPT

Caste in India

This story touches on some of the complex issues related to caste, the traditional system which influences all individuals of Hindu society affecting occupation, marriage, and social standing. This story, in a number of ways, draws out some of the characteristics and tensions of this social system in today's India, where modern education and urban mobility have created changes in the way the system works.

Traditionally one's caste or, to use the more precise Hindi word, *jati,* determined occupation, and to some extent this is still true. Examples of this from the story are the characters, Ganga and her mother, who are from the *ahir* or cow herder *jati,* whose members raise cows and buffalo, process and sell the products of these animals: milk, yoghurt, *ghee,* cow dung, etc. Another character, Beni Tamoli, is a *paan* vendor by caste, and this is the work he does in the story. Like the occupations of these characters, many of the more traditional occupations visible today on the streets and ghats of Banaras are done almost exclusively by a particular *jati* or by a few castes, namely boatmen, barbers, temple priests, laundrymen, and many more. However, increasingly people have found jobs in occupations created by India's modernization that have little to do with their traditional ancestral work. For example, Sidhua Kahar of this story works as a laborer in a factory, not as a kahar who traditionally works as a household servant and a carrier of palanquins.

Jatis in India number in the thousands, and each one may be characterized by a separate set of rules governing acceptable behavior for its members. Despite this variation of customs from one caste to the next, however, one *jati*-related custom that is nearly universal in India is that of endogamy, or marriage within the *jati.* As long as the vast majority of Indian marriages are arranged, the tradition of parents' choosing someone from within their own caste as their child's spouse is likely to remain the rule.

Although endogamy is common to most jatis, other customs vary. For example, a woman's ability to remarry after widowhood or abandonment—an issue raised in this story—differs among *jatis.* In general remarriage is not allowed among the higher *jatis,* those

163

considered to be part of the first three of the four levels of society, or *varnas,* laid down in the Vedas: Brahmin, Kshatriya, and Vaisha.

The notion of *jati* and hierarchy—or, to put it another way, the issue of systematic inequality—is perhaps the most controversial aspect of this uniquely Indian social system; it is this issue which the author brings up in connection with his mention in the story of "dharma." In its widest sense, *dharma* refers to the universal laws of nature that uphold the cosmos. Here it refers more narrowly to the code of conduct of a *jati.* This *jati dharma* is the practice which leads to proper behavior and moral conduct through the observance of *jati* rules which define an individual's responsibility and moral obligations. Only within the *jati* framework should the obligations of *dharma* be observed. The *Bhagavad-gita*, for example, teaches that to do one's own duty even badly is morally superior to performing another's duty well. Hence to treat someone as if they are so low as to have no *jati dharma* is to rob them of their dignity—of their role in society. This is what Ganga and Beni discuss towards the end of this story.

Figure 9.—This river festival held to honor Lord Ganesh was included in Louis Rousselet's, *L'Inde Des Rajahs*, published in 1875. Like the Burva Manga Mela of the following story, this river festival displayed the elaborate exuberance of an old-fashioned good time in Banaras.

12

The Drowsiness of Chait Dulls the Spirit

Introduction

At the beginning of this story the author introduces the Burva Mangal Mela. Dating from the early 1700s, this mela, *or fair, is a near-legendary event, a four-day, musical extravaganza that used to be held on boats anchored in the middle of the Ganges. Perhaps the fair's origin so long ago accounts for the enigmatic name which literally means "old Thursday" or "old joy." Memories of the fair from its last years in the 1920s leave us with a vivid idea of how it was celebrated. For the wealthy of the city, the fair was an occasion to ostentatiously display their social position, as well as to share generous amounts of food,* paan, bhang, *and alcohol. Many accounts tell of the dancing women and singers, the other small boats selling flowers, sweets and other accessories, and of the final, all-night music festival at the Maharajah's palace.*[1]

*The fair's decline probably resulted from a change in the sense of decorum in matters relating to the public display of wealth. Perhaps the growing popularity of the independence movement's socialist values made the idea of the elite of the city lavishly and openly enjoying themselves seem in bad taste. Today, however, the Burva Mangal is remembered fondly for its association with an old-fashioned sense of what it meant to have a good time in Banaras. The joys of yesteryear—*bhang, paan, *classical, and folk music, excursions to the countryside, and an easy, laid-back* musti *attitude toward life—seem to be increasingly replaced by films and their popular music, television, and liquor.*

---

[1] Vishwanath Mukherjee, *Yah Banaras Hai*, Varanasi, Vishwavidyalay Prakashen, 1973, pp. 61-67, and Nita Kumar, *The Artisans of Banaras*, Princeton University Press, 1988, pp. 127-131.

The title of this story comes from a Bhairavi, *a type of classical music sung only in the morning. The* Chait *of the title refers to the Hindu month which falls in March/April. This is a special time of the year when the weather starts to change from the coolness of winter to the heat of summer. Neither too cold, nor too hot, the weather of Chait is ideal for nighttime activities such as fairs, singing contests, and even lovemaking. The reference in the title to the drowsiness of Chait is a reference to the after-effect of all this nocturnal activity and the increasing heat.*

Words and phrases in italics are explained in a glossary at the end of this story. Also, a postscript to this story, found after the glossary, contains notes on Harischandra Ghat, Bharatendu Harischandra, and the significance of drinking Ganges water at the point of death.

(1)

The 78-year-old *Pundit* Padmanand Pandey had spent the night writhing in bed like a badly-wounded fawn. To forget his anxiety, he stepped out on his roof into the southerly wind of dawn and started to pace. He noticed that, even in spring, dark rain clouds had started to fill the sky. In the distance, the *Burva Mangal Mela* was rolling on the waves of the Ganges. He tried to see the festival, but with his dim eyesight, he could only make out scattered, reflected light on the water.

Then he heard the melodious tone of a *Bhairavi*, penetrating the canopy of air, clashing with his ear drum: "The youth of one's life is a companion for only a few days!"

Padmanand, agreeing with the statement of the woman singer, shook his head and said, "It's true, the joy of one's youth is short-lived!" and his stooped back bent even more.

On the floor below, his young woman tenant, Ganga, had come to sweep the courtyard. The dawn's darkness slowly decreased; the sky became red. Padmanand descended the steps entering the courtyard. Recognizing the sound of his footsteps, the two cows tied there perked up their ears; a weak mooing sound issued from their mouths. Padmanand entered the courtyard and stood staring for some time at the two large-framed, but bony,

167

cows—Nandani and Kamdhenu. He took a deep breath and went into a long, wide room next door where the fodder was stored and looked around. In one corner, at most half a kilo of straw was mixed with dirt and mud. He sifted out about four fistfuls and added a liter-and-a-half of water in the cows' troughs. Immediately, the two broke excitedly for the anticipated meal. A moment later, however, they lifted their heads to look at Padmanand. Tears came to his eyes, as if to say, "I myself have been hungry for several days, mother cows! What can I do?"

Meanwhile, Ganga was sweeping in front of her room in the courtyard, and at the same time, noticing out of the corner of her eyes what was happening to Padmanand. She saw his tears—quickly wiped away with a tattered cloth. Approaching him hesitatingly, she said, "Sir, this month has already started. For several days, I've been thinking that I should pay the rent in advance; but I haven't had any money. Now it's come. Should I give it?" Padmanand remained silent. Ganga went into her room and returned. Handing over a five-rupee note, she said to Padmanand, "Sir, take it all. Two-and-a-half rupees are for this month and two-and-a-half for next month."

Padmanand, taking the money, asked, "You don't have five more rupees, do you? I need ten very badly."

Ganga said softly, "I really don't have any more, but wait here a minute." She called out, "Hey, Gango, has your mother returned from bathing?" Hearing Ganga's call, a five- or six-year-old girl came out of another room in the courtyard. She answered, "Yes, sister, mother's back. She's counting her prayer beads. What is it?"

Instead of answering, Ganga went to Gango's mother and, handing over her silver bangles said, "Loan me five rupees. You can hold on to these for security, mother of Gango. In a month, we'll settle and I'll give you two paise for every rupee in interest."

Hearing about the two paise for every rupee, Gango's mother could not refuse. If Ganga had not mentioned the interest and, instead, had just asked for a loan of five rupees, surely Gango's mother would have straightaway answered, "I keep all my money in Rai Sahib's house. He won't give it to me without a good reason. He'll say that, after I die, the money is for Gango." But she was not able to resist the chance of effortlessly earning ten paise every month, so she took Ganga's bangles and gave her the money. When Ganga handed it over to Padmanand, the old man's face lit up, and he left the house right away.

(2)

As if he'd attached feathers to his feet, the old man flew through the twisted lanes of *Kashi.* Seeing him hastily leave the house, Ganga thought he was going to get food for himself and fodder for his cows. So, she would surely have been surprised to see that the old man, raised at a time when people did what they said, was not going to the markets at Vishesvarganj or Khojwa where the city's main food supply centers were located. Rather, his aim was a dilapidated house in one dark lane. When the old man got there, he rattled the hasp on the door. Immediately, a heavy woman with peppered hair and a few broken teeth opened the door and asked, "Did you bring the money?"

"Yes, I've brought it," Padmanand answered placing the two 5-rupee notes in the woman's outstretched hands, "but how did you know I was bringing it?"

"Oh, I knew you'd bring it," the old woman answered, choking with affection.

The two of the them were standing in the sunset of their lives. Both of them knew that the dusk of the great night of death was in front of them. Nonetheless, their conversation was colored with youthful affection, filling their empty hearts like dawn's first hopeful rays. Padmanand laughed and asked, "Tell me how you knew that I'd bring you this money without your even asking for it? Tell me how you knew that I'd come to this door in spite of

169

having been insulted so often by your sons, Bal Ram and Bakheru?"

The old woman laughed heartily, and then like a young girl, she teased him with the words of the poet *Bihari:* "She says, 'yes,' but then....no!" Then, getting serious, she said, "Well, you! How were you able to know? You're a man, aren't you? Men only see the outer beauty. But a woman has intuition. She doesn't only see outside, but she can peek inside, as well. You get my point?"

"Even if he didn't get the point before, I'll make sure he gets it now," said Bakheru Ram, who had come from his room threatening with a shoe raised in one hand.

Bakheru Ram was born hating his mother, Sonamati. His father, Buddhi Dutt Pandey, on the other hand, was an idiot from the day he was born, and easy to deceive. But his mother! In his own words, she was nobody's fool, and so she blocked his freedom. Fortunately for Bakheru Ram, from his childhood, he had known something about his mother that had given him the confidence of a lion in dealing with her.

Almost 50 years ago, when this Sonamati, at the age of 15, was married, she had gone to live in the house of her husband's younger cousin—this old Padmanand. At that time, several events occurred in the family. First, there was the sudden death of Padmanand's wife. The rumor was that she had killed herself. Even though Padmanand had disposed of most of his wealth, spending lavishly on music and other artistic events, enough money remained for him to marry again. Nonetheless, he surprised everyone and refused to remarry.

A few days after this decision not to remarry was made, Buddhi Dutt, who had been very dependent for money on his cousin, Padmanand, *refused to stay in the family house* and went out to rent another place.

In spite of Buddhi Dutt's move, Padmanand started to go to his cousin's house and to receive the same respect he always received from his cousin's wife, Sonamati. To society at large, this relationship was viewed with distaste; but to Bakheru Ram it was like a weapon to pierce his mother's heart.

Recently, Buddhi Dutt was taken sick. There was no money to send him for treatment. But the insolent Bakheru Ram, not understanding the generosity of Padmanand, was now attacking him with his shoe. The old Padmanand broke out crying. Sonamati enraged, shouted, "Look you fool. You just hit your own father with a shoe! Your father is not Buddhi Dutt Pandey. He's impotent," the old woman shouted. Bakheru Ram was shocked, and his distraction allowed Padmanand to slip away.

(3)

Mumbling to himself insanely, Padmanand wandered all day. At sunset, he went to Harischandra Ghat and watched a group of children playing a game on steps they had hacked out of the mud deposited by the Ganges's flood.

Standing on the highest step, a girl asked, "Fish, fish, how deep is the water?"

A group of boys and girls standing on the lowest steps answered, putting both their hands on their waists, "Hey, golden bird, the water comes up to here."

The lone girl standing above came down one step. She asked again, "Hey, fish, how deep is the water?" The girl, who was playing the part of the golden bird, like a poet reciting couplets, kept repeating her question after descending each step. Meanwhile at the bottom, the boys and girls who were playing the fish gave the required answer to the question by placing their hands respectively on their ribs, stomachs, waists, thighs, knees, etc., to indicate the rising level of water.

All this noise did not please Padmanand. He turned away and looked with his dim eyesight at the river Ganges. He saw large waves pounding in the river and boats tossing around. The strong gusts of wind on his loose skin reminded him of the *Burva Mangal Mela,* when all the boats were tied to one another. At that time, he remembered, not even a year had passed since his father's death. His own boat had attracted the most attention in the procession, except for those of the Maharajah of Kashi and the Rajah of Vijaynagaram. Then again, a crisp gust of wind came and Padmanand, seated on the shore, got wet. The wave was not just a wave of the Ganges, it was also a swell in the ocean of his memory. The description of the Burva Mangel Mela, which had been printed in a monthly publication of Bharatendu Harischandra, came into his mumbling mouth. Because he quoted that description every day for three straight years, it was etched in his heart forever. He started to recite:

"In the last Burva Mangal, something unprecedented and memorable happened. It was on Friday, the day of the festival, when the wind was blowing at such a speed that it dispersed the procession of boats, making it impossible for them to reach Ramnagar. The yacht of the Maharajah of Vijaynagaram was stuck on this side of the river. But when the Maharajah of Kashi saw that the splendid yachts were not able to move forward, he summoned his elephants. As soon as the command was given, the greatest elephants—swaying together—went into the Ganges. Some pulled with their tusks. Some butted with their heads. Some pushed with their rumps, and some grabbed the side of the yachts and pulled with their trunks. You had to see this spectacle to really appreciate it; words are not adequate to describe it."

Pundit Padmanand's mind started to bob in the excitement of his memories. His poverty had kept him in a partial fast for several months. His immoral youth had created awful problems for his weak old age; but even today his eternally youthful heart was longing for the old, colorful ways. The fire of hunger in his stomach increased the sparks dancing before his eyes. Taking refuge in the Ganges's waters to extinguish the flame, he

172

struggled to drink a few handfuls of water. His stomach suddenly cramped and he sat down to rest, pained.

"Fish, fish, how deep is the water?" received the customary answer: "Golden Bird, the water is this deep." And the girl, with a thud, jumped down to the bottom step. The boys and girls in the role of fish gathered around the newly arrived golden bird. At first the golden bird, pretending to flap her wings, moved her arms quickly, but then, abandoning the effort to escape, her arms fell slack.

On the stone steps, Pundit Padmanand died.

Frantically looking for him like someone crazed, Sonamati arrived at the ghat. Bystanders had gathered around. One asked, "Is he dead or what? Why isn't he getting up?"

Sonamati was just about to answer when from some distant boat, a singer, unaware of this incident, sang out, "The drowsiness of Chait dulls the spirit, Oh Ram!"

GLOSSARY

(in order of appearance in the text)

Pundit—a title of respect applied to learned people, often associated with learned Brahmins.

Kashi—"the City of Light," the most ancient of the many names for Banaras.

Bihari—Bihari Lal, a seventeenth-century poet renowned for his amorous dialogues between Krishna and Radha.

Refused to stay in the family house—In other words, refused, seemingly because a romantic relationship had developed between Sonamati and Padmanand, to abide by the extended family custom of several paternally connected families living together under the same roof.

POSTSCRIPT

Harischandra Ghat

Today, this is one of the two burning ghats on Banaras' river shore where cremations daily take place. It is considered by many to be the more holy even though, since the construction of an electric crematorium in 1987, few traditional funeral pyres are lighted at Harischandra Ghat these days. The pilgrims who come to Banaras know the story of the king after whom the ghat is named and frequently wish to see the images depicting his life, which are painted on a temple at the river's edge.

The truthful King Harischandra once angered the zealous sage Visvamitra. To placate him, the king offered the sage anything he might ask for. Seizing the opportunity, Visvamitra took everything from Harischandra: his kingdom, his wife and son, and finally, the King's own freedom, requiring that Harischandra sell himself into slavery and give Visvamitra the money from his sale.

Harischandra's slave-master was a chief of the *doms,* an untouchable caste that traditionally oversees the degrading and ritually polluting work at cremation grounds. His master sent Harischandra to Banaras to carry out this defiling work and to steal the shrouds off dead bodies. One day, after a year of this, his wife arrived carrying their son who had been killed by a cobra bite. When Harischandra and his wife were about to leap onto their son's funeral pyre, the gods, led by Indra, intervened, and, recognizing the king's honesty and humility, allowed him, his wife, and followers to ascend to heaven.

Bharatendu Harischandra

Born in Banaras in 1850, Bharatendu Harischandra is often called the "father of modern Hindi." In many respects, the life of the main character of this story, Padmanand, is like that of Bharatendu Harischandra. Like the character, Bharatendu came from a wealthy family; and he spent his inheritance lavishly on literary and cultural activities, as well as on more hedonistic pursuits. His generosity and his seeming indifference to maintaining his wealth have often led to comparisons with his namesake, King Harischandra. He was also typical of those who propagated the lifestyle reflected in the ostentation and feudal flavor of the *Burva Mangal Mela*. Most importantly, Bharatendu Harischandra is renowned as an energetic poet, dramatist, and essayist who laid the foundation for modern Hindi, establishing schools, literary societies, and two magazines, one of which is referred to in this story. For this, he has been known by the name, "Bharatendu," or "Moon of India."[1]

Significance of Drinking Water from the Ganges before Death

The Ganga's ability to cleanse sins and thereby bring a dying person closer to liberation is well known. Tradition holds that the goddess Ganga will embrace even those whose life conduct, as judged by conventional standards, is unfit for salvation. If fate itself should bring the dying person to the Ganges to drink, as happens in the story, then this is clearly auspicious, and perhaps reflects the writer's judgement about the individual's conduct.

---

[1] Kathryn Hansen, "The Birth of Hindi Drama in Banaras, 1868-1885," in Sandria B. Freitag, ed., *Culture and Power in Banaras*, University of California Press, Berkeley, 1989, pp.78-92.

Figure 10.—This sketch, "Religious Beggars in Benares" appeared in Louis Rousselet's *L'Inde Des Rajahs* published in 1875, and draws attention to a group of *sadhus* like the one which appears in the following story. .

13

The Words of the Devas and the Rishis Will Never Fail

Introduction

Two tales are woven together in this story. We enter the first at about the time of India's independence in 1947. The second takes us back to the seventeenth century, to one of the many extraordinary accounts of Kina Ram, a tantric saint, born in 1658 near Banaras.

The story title, attributed erroneously by the Sadhu character in the story to the Bhagavad-gita, *is really a popular expression from the Ram Charit Manas of Tulsi Das (referred to in the first story of this collection).* Devas *refers to the major deities of the Hindu pantheon and* Rishis *were the sages who possessed extraordinary power and wisdom. The story opens in Nagwa, a small, suburban community on the shore of the Ganges, south of the city and north of Banaras Hindu University. The fort of the Maharajah of Banaras faces Nagwa on the far shore of the Ganges in Ramnagar.*

Words and phrases in italics are explained in a glossary at the end of the story. Also, a postscript to this story, found after the glossary, contains notes on Kina Ram's curse, Shaivite symbolism, Kina Ram's life, Aghoris, and Bahari Alang.

Sukkhu was sitting at Nagwa *Ghat,* washing off the grinding stone and stone slab with clean water. He set the long, cylindrical grinding stone upright on the slab and poured the milky *bhang* from the shell of a coconut onto it. While doing so, he chanted, "Accept this, oh *Bholenath!"*

His companion, Jhingur, had been diving in the water, looking for a piece of soap that had slipped from his hands. As he climbed out of the water, he recited the *Vijaya mantra,* the last part of which he shouted: "The goddess Kali will eat up whoever talks disparagingly of *bhang."* Then he turned to Sukkhu and asked, "Hey, brother Sukkhu, is it ready yet?"

"It's been ready for some time. I've just been waiting till you got out of the water."

"I still need a little more time, friend!"

"Fine, I'll put your share aside and take mine now."

Jhingur shook his head approvingly, and Sukkhu filled his coconut shell with *bhang,* getting ready to drink. Just as the coconut shell reached his lips, he heard a voice from behind him, "Hey, son, drinking alone are you?"

Sukkhu turned and saw the impressive figure of a saintly man, standing grinning from ear to ear, clearly desiring to be included. A saffron robe was swaying over his body. In one hand, he had the wooden water pot of a *sadhu* and in the other a metal *trishul* covered with red *sindur* powder. His head was covered with earth-caked hair, and his beard reached down to his navel. This exotic figure impressed Sukkhu, who answered, "Why not? Everything is due to your power, *guruji.* Where is your *ashram, Maharaj?"*

"A Sadhu is always on the move, my son! He has no fixed place. As the saint *Kabir Das* said:
'A *sadhu* is better off when he's like running water,
never merging into an ocean.
The moment he becomes stationary, he turns into stone
or into a miserable pond.' "

179

The *sadhu* wasn't able to finish his poem; Jhingur, squeezing the water from his *dhoti* on a stone, said, "Hey, where did that odd crow come from?"

The *sadhu* looked at Jhingur bitterly, but stayed quiet. Sukkhu answered, "Watch your language. He's a great soul, a mahatma. He saw us here and came over."

Completely ignoring Jhingur, the *sadhu* addressed Sukkhu, "What's the delay, son? Give me some bhang, won't you?"

"Here take it, *babaji*. Should I put it in your water pot?"

"Yes, yes, put it in here."

The Sadhu pushed his pot forward, and Sukkhu put a little bhang in it. The Sadhu downed the bhang in one deep gulp, and then took a small bundle of *ganja* and a long brass *chillum* from his robe. He started to rub a bit of the *ganja* with the thumb of one hand in the palm of the other. Meanwhile Jhingur had spread out his *dhoti* to dry and came up to them. When he saw that only a little bhang remained, he scowled, "Hey, Sukkhu, have you also been taken in by this holy nonsense?"

Sukkhu answered, "Oh, my friend, we should only take this after offering it to the Sadhu. Then it's like *prasad.*"

"Oh, stop. I've seen so many *sadhus* like this one. Look at him, does he seem like a real one?"

Meanwhile the *sadhu* had rubbed the *ganja* and fired up his *chillum* with some tobacco. He took a few quick puffs and stared, red-eyed, at Jhingur. Jhingur met his stare and said, "Don't show me this fake anger, or you might come to regret it."

"You shall be destroyed," the *sadhu* snarled his curse.

"Watch your tongue," Jhingur said angrily.

"Are you insulting a *sadhu?* You will be de-de-de-destroyed," the Sadhu stammered.

"Why are you keeping it up, still pretending to be some great baba! Don't you know that the very stones of Kashi are Shiva's?* Your curses don't scare me."

"Who are you? Even the great are afraid of curses. Haven't you heard what is written in the Gita? 'The words of the Devas and the Rishis will never fail'."

"I've seen so many phonies."

"You haven't seen a thing. If you want to see something, look in front of you on the other side of the river at Ramnagar. There you can see what a Sadhu's curse can do."

Jhingur's gaze followed the Sadhu's pointing finger to the other side of the river, toward the Maharajah's fort. As though it was already *Dipawali*, the entire fort was bathed in light. It was sunset on the eighth day of the waning fortnight in the month of *Kartik*. In the west, the sun had already set. But in the east, the moon had not yet appeared. The darkness of evening had spread. The fort, brightly lighted against the black background, looked like a picture, showing the face of a beautiful woman surrounded by the deep darkness of black hair.

By this time, Jhingur had lost the energy to argue. He kept looking, spellbound, at the fort. A thin line of a smile appeared on the Sadhu's face, making him look even more saintly; and this brought Sukkhu to venerate him all the more. In an extremely humble voice, he asked, "Maharaj, how are the Rajah's fort and a Sadhu's curse related?"

"They are closely related, my son. I have noticed that you are a respectful and reverent person, so I'll explain everything to you. Have you ever heard the name of the Rajah, Chait Singh, my son?"

"Yes, sir, of course I know it well. He was the son of Rajah Balwant Singh, wasn't he? And this fort in front of us was his."

---

* See glossary

"Yes, exactly. You are indeed very knowledgeable, my boy. Yes, so this goes back to the time of Chait Singh. When he was the king of Banaras, there was a very famous saint resident in *Kashi,* my son."

"Who was that, *guruji*?" Sukkhu asked reverently with his hands folded in front of him.

"Baba Kina Ram."

"Baba Kina Ram!" Sukkhu said with a mixture of joy and astonishment, "I know a lot about Baba Kina Ram, guru. Even today my mother recites prayers and songs written by him. So then what happened, maharaj?"

"Yes, my son. So, in the shadow of this fort one day, the Rajah Chait Singh was taking a walk. From the other side, this Baba Kina Ram happened to show up. When the Rajah saw him, he became arrogant, like your friend here, and didn't even greet him. Baba stopped. Saints have no ego, my son. Just as I came to you and begged from you, so, too, Kina Ram said to the Rajah, 'Rajah, I'm hungry.' The Rajah looked at him and said with a hate-filled smile, 'Wait here. I'll order some food for you.' The Rajah signalled one of his servants to come. He was a scribe—a very clever man. Are you following me, son?"

Sukkhu was listening to the words of the Sadhu with great respect. He was getting the essence of the story, even though some of the details escaped him. He bowed his head and said, "Yes Maharaj, I understand."

"You don't understand anything, my boy. The thing to understand is yet to be told. Now pay attention." So the scribe folded his hands and said to the Rajah, 'Rajah, don't make an enemy of the *sadhu.'* But the Rajah paid no attention. He said, 'I'm a *kshatriya,* the Sadhu is also a *kshatriya.* But I'm the king, and he's a beggar. Why didn't he greet me?' "

"Shame, shame. This was the level of the king's wisdom?" Sukkhu supported humbly.

"Yes, my boy. That's the thing. *Surdas* has said, 'After you have missed the chance, it's too late to repent.' So, the scribe again said, 'OK, then let me go and get *babaji's* food.' The Rajah said, 'Yes, go get it. But look, this afternoon a dead body floated up on the shore, on the other side of the fort. It's foul smelling. Have the *doms* bring it up here.' "

"What!" Sukkhu opened his mouth with astonishment and kept it open for a full minute.

The *sadhu* smiled as before and went on, "So the scribe said, 'Sir, you can take my life, but this kind of thing I can't do.' Baba Kina Ram stood there hearing everything. He said, 'Sada-anand, do as he says; and, by the way, I give your family the name which means "forever blissful," so in your family always add "anand" to your names, and they will be forever blessed. Then the newly named 'Sada-anand' quickly had the body brought up to the scene.

"The Rajah said to the *sadhu*, 'Start eating!' All the attendants and servants standing there turned their heads away in disgust. The Rajah scolded them, so they turned back and looked at the awful scene in front of them. The Sadhu took his shawl and placed it over the corpse. Five minutes later, he said to Sada-anand, 'Remove the shawl.' Sada-anand, shaking with fear, approached the body and removed the shawl,with his eyes shut. He heard cheers and, when he opened his eyes, what did he see?" the *sadhu* asked Sukkhu, as if he were talking to a child.

Sukkhu was scared. What should he say? Then he got the idea that the *sadhu* must have been angered by what the Rajah had done. So he said slowly, "The corpse must have become a python."

"Not quite, my son!" The Sadhu laughed loudly with affection and said, "No, not a python, son. It turned into fine delicacies, fine sweets—laddhu, pera, barfi, jelebi, imarti, mohanbhog, etc." While he was talking, the *sadhu* started to pant from excitement, but he continued: "When the Rajah saw the

183

sadhu's miracle, he realized the truth. Frightened, he fell at the *sadhu's* feet, but the *sadhu* said, 'No! No longer can you remain Rajah. And do you know who will dethrone you? This scribe, Sada-anand!' The Rajah trembled, my son. He begged and begged. Then the Sadhu softened. He said, 'You have to abandon the throne, but because of your supplication, I have become pleased and will therefore declare that after you, the descendants of your glorious father will receive a fractured kingdom. And then, after ruling for six generations, your kingdom will be dissolved.'*

The ever-reverent Sukkhu did not understand what the Sadhu meant by the word "dissolved," and he wasn't able to get a question out about the relationship between that idea and the decorations visible on the other side of the river.

Jhingur laughed, "*Sadhuji,* are you stoned?" The Sadhu turned and stared at him. Jhingur just kept on laughing.

Ever since the *sadhu* had pointed to the decorated fort, Jhingur, too, had been wondering why the fort was so lit up today. The *sadhu's* loud peal of laughter, when Sukkhu mentioned the python, had interrupted Jhingur's concentration, and after that, he didn't catch whatever had come out of the *baba's* mouth. He was curious and started to laugh.

"But Maharaj," Sukkhu asked, "What do you mean by dissolved?"

Then from somewhere a whistle sounded. The *sadhu* was startled. He said, sitting up, "This means that from today Chait Singh's rule is coming to an end. The government in Delhi is giving control of the kingdom to the state government in Lucknow. You understand, my son?" With this, the *sadhu* moved on. Just as he turned the corner, he saw a senior police officer and some of his underlings. He looked around him and then gave a

---

* See glossary

military salute to the police officer. The officer said, "Well, *babaji,* you execute your duties very carefully!"

"I've already told you, sir, 'The words of the *devas* and the *rishis* will never fail.' From you, there is nothing to hide, sir." the Sadhu said.

"That's what I always say," the officer said. "You really can't hide anything from me. So taking *ganja* and *bhang* and talking whatever nonsense you've been blubbering is completely out of line. Do you know what the punishment is for breaking the rules?"

"If you say so, sir, it must be right. 'The words of the *devas* and the *rishis* will never fail,' Sitaram, Sitaram!" The *sadhu* said this benediction loudly, and then a few other men could be seen turning the corner and approaching the officer and the *sadhu.* The officer went off in another direction, smiling to himself at the cleverness of his senior secret policeman.

Back on the bank of the river, Jhingur asked suddenly when he heard the *sadhu,* "Isn't today the 15th?"

"How should I know? Anyway, what's supposed to happen on the 15th?"

"Sukkhu, you really are an idiot!" Jhingur said with a smile. Sukkhu also smiled, even though he didn't understand.

A loud, happy sound came from the direction of the fort. Jhingur joined Sukkhu, staring at the fort. He kept looking toward the room that was known to be the Rajah's. Suddenly he saw someone come and stand in the window. Keeping his eyes pinned to that figure, he said to his companion, "Hey, the Rajah is standing in front of us. We should say, 'Har, har, mahadev.' "*
But, then he thought a little and said, "But if there is no longer a kingdom...?"

"You mean," Sukkhu said to Jhingur, "if there's no longer a kingdom, then that man is not king any more? But if a temple is

---

* See glossary

185

destroyed, does the deity also disappear? You can keep quiet if you want!" And then Sukkhu looked toward that window and shouted, "Har, har, mahadev!"[*]

---

[*] See glossary

GLOSSARY

Ghat—steps leading down to a river.

Bhang—an intoxicating drink made from hemp.

Bholenath—a name for Shiva which literally means "the simple hearted (Bhola) lord (nath)," and refers to Shiva's good, gentle, easy-to-please, intoxicated nature.

Vijaya mantra—the sacred victory verse of the goddess Kali.

Sadhu—an ascetic, holy person who is supposed to have renounced all worldly possessions.

Trishul—Shiva's weapon, a long spear with three prongs on the end, a trident.

Sindur—a red powder used to anoint images of deities and sacred objects.

Guruji—a teacher or spiritual guide, and in Banaras, a widely used term of respect.

Ashram—a religious retreat.

Maharaj—a term of respect and authority.

Kabir Das—Kabir Das was a fifteenth-century poet—a Muslim weaver, perhaps a convert to Islam from a low caste Hindu family—who lived in Banaras and condemned in the most ardent terms the pretensions of holy men of all religions.

Dhoti—the traditional dress of north Indian men, consisting of a white, ankle-length cloth elaborately wrapped around the waist.

Babaji—a title of respect.

Ganja—an intoxicant, like *bhang*, from the hemp plant.

Chillum—a small, clay pipe used for smoking *ganja* or hashish.

Prasad—food or other offering to a deity after which, in the case of food, it stands consecrated to the offerer.

"The very stones of Kashi are Shiva's"—a common saying in Banaras (also referred to as Kashi) that means Shiva's presence is everywhere in the holy city and his power is not just the prerogative of a few.

Dipawali—a Hindu festival, a kind of New Year's day when houses are repainted, merchants start a new fiscal year, and in general people celebrate by placing rows of lighted oil lamps around the outside of homes.

Kartik—October/November.

Kashi—"The City of Light," the most ancient of the many names for Banaras.

Kshatriya—Kshatriya is one of the four varnas or castes. From top to bottom, the four, along with their traditional occupations, are brahmans (priests), kshatriyas (warrior-kings), vaishas (merchants-artisans-landowners), and shudras (servants).

Surdas—a blind poet, a devotee of Krishna, who lived in the fifteenth century near Agra. Like the title of this story which the Sadhu mistakenly attributes to the *Bhagavad Gita*, he has also misattributed this quote, trying to appear more knowledgeable than he is.

Dom—A caste whose traditional occupation is to work at the cremation grounds.

Dissolved—a reference to the dissolution of the princely states that took place at the time of independence.

"Har, har, mahadev"—a slogan which means "Hail to the great Lord Shiva." The slogan is still often shouted when the Maharajah of Banaras—the earthly representative of Shiva—appears in public.

POSTSCRIPT

Kina Ram's Curse

As described in the first story, many believe the raja's family is cursed. In the earlier story, the Rajah's wife issues the curse that every other generation will have to adopt a son in order to continue ruling. In this story, the curse predicts Chait Singh's flight from the British (the background to the second story), the "fracturing" of the kingdom with the loss of Banaras, and the loss that the rajahs and maharajahs suffered with independence when the princely states were "dissolved," (to use the words of the *sadhu,)* and absorbed by the state governments.

Shaivite Symbolism

The opening of the story is full of Shaivite symbolism, taking the reader into a special context from the outset connected with the god Shiva. Because most tantrics are followers of Shiva and his consorts, this opening material serves the purpose of anticipating the tantric material that follows. For example, in the process of placing the grinding stone upright and pouring milky *bhang* over it, the ritual of pouring milk over a *shiva lingam* (the symbolic phallus of Shiva worshiped all over India) is re-created so that Shiva will bless their taking of *bhang,* his favorite intoxicant. This image is enhanced when Shiva is invoked by the name "Bholenath," which literally means "the simple hearted (Bhola) lord (nath)," and refers to Shiva's gentle, easy-to-please, intoxicated nature.

Another reference is Jhingur's reciting the "Vijaya mantra" or sacred victory verse of the goddess Kali. When Kali is associated with a god as consort, she is almost always connected with Shiva. She is usually depicted as a fierce, bellicose goddess, invoked for success against one's enemies. As a figure of death and destruction, Kali is often associated with tantric worship and hence is connected with Kina Ram.

Another Shaivite image in the story is the ascetic who is described as carrying one of the most important symbols of Shiva—the trishul, a long spear with three prongs on the end, like a trident. This is Shiva's weapon, carried by Sadhus who are his devotees.

189

Many of the events of Kina Ram's life are connected with his magical powers, acquired through spiritual exercises early in his life—almost, it seems, from birth. As a boy, he resisted involvement in worldly affairs, desiring instead to focus his energies on matters of the spirit in preparation for becoming a *sadhu*. This resistance took on such intensity that, at the age of 15 his parents, concerned about his premature other-worldliness, insisted that he marry. Forced to give in to his family's demands, he turned to his extraordinary powers for salvation. The day before the new bride was to come to his home, the young Kina Ram ordered his mother to prepare a milk and rice dish. Believing this to be an inauspicious combination, his mother argued with him to eat yoghurt and rice. In the end, the boy prevailed. Shortly after he ate his milk and rice, the news of his bride's death reached the house, and Kina Ram was free of family pressure.

Aghoris

Kina Ram's life and beliefs are often connected with a symbol believed by conventional Hinduism to be most defiling and inauspicious—a human corpse. This connection with death has brought Kina Ram into association with a group of ascetics called the *aghoris,* who claim Kina Ram as the founder of their order. *aghoris,* like other Hindu sects that may be grouped together in a tradition called tantrism, believe that the way to liberation comes from inverting the ordinary symbols and values of Hinduism and, in a very physical way, uniting opposites such as life and death so that one may move beyond them and identify with the supreme reality. Hence, what conventional Hindus proscribe and find inauspicious and repellent is considered pure, auspicious, and valuable by *aghoris* and other followers of tantric practices. For example, *aghoris* are said to seat themselves on the torso of a corpse to worship. In so doing, they are supposed to be able to obtain control over the corpse's spirit, and are able to communicate with the dead. They use the ashes of the funeral pyre to cook, and they eat and drink out of the human skull of someone who died prematurely. Furthermore, *aghoris* are said to eat and drink almost anything: alcohol, urine, excrement, even the putrid flesh of corpses. Those who are successful in these practices are said to attain fantastic powers, as Kina Ram demonstrates in this story.[1]

One of the centers of *aghori* belief is Kina Ram's ashram, located in Ravendrapuri in southern Banaras. Within the compound walls, conspicuously dotted with clay images of skulls, one can visit Kina Ram's tomb and bathe in the pool of Kina Ram, believed to relieve a follower of certain diseases. This is also where a holy fire burns, kept alive by logs donated from the funeral pyres of Banaras—a custom said to have been initiated under the seventeenth-century Moghul emperor Shah Jahan. Though the number of *aghori* ascetics in Banaras is currently very low, these few are well known and have a large following.

Bahari Alang

This story introduces one of Banaras' quintessential re-creations, a type of outing called *bahari alang*.[2] Though the outing can take several forms, certain activities are essential and some of these appear in the story, such as bathing in the Ganges or in a pool, washing clothes, and grinding and eating *bhang*. Another near-essential activity for *bahari alang* is relieving oneself in nature, perhaps popularized by the overcrowded conditions of the city and the general Indian distaste for cramped latrines. Usually *bahari alang* is celebrated by a group of male friends, and sometimes includes cooking and eating a meal prepared in clay pots over burning cow dung cakes. One of the most popular spots for *bahari alang* is on the sandy east shore of the Ganges, opposite the city.

---

[1] Jonathan P. Perry, "The Aghori Ascetics of Benares," in Richard Burghart and Audry Cantlie, eds, *Indian Religion*, St. Martins Press, New York, 1985, pp. 51-78.

[2] For a good description of *bahari alang*, see Nita Kumar, *The Artisans of Banaras; Popular Culture and Identity, 1880-1986*, Princeton University Press, 1988, especially Chapter 4, "The Other Side."

BFI
OTHER WORKS FROM BOOK FAITH INDIA

SHIVA

Beautiful coloured photographs and descriptive text illustrates the multifarious aspects of the personality of Shiva, believed by Hindus to be the destroyer of the universe and considered the most important god of the Hindu pantheon. The authors vividly describe Shiva's yogic powers, sexuality, and relationships with his consort and family. "A fascinating account of Hinduism and its unfathomable mythology."

133 pages. Paperback. Colour photographs.

US $16.00 Item No. 974-86974-3-6 Shipping: $1.50

THE YOGA APHORISMS OF PATANJALI

translation by William Q. Judge

A classic reprint of Patanjali's *Yoga Sutras* originally published by The Theosophical Society, Bombay, 1885. "An essential gem for anyone interested in yoga."

74 pages. Paperback.

US $2.95 Item No. 045. Shipping: $0.50

THE PSALM OF SIVA'S GLORY

translation by R.N. Tiwari

The composer of this holy hymn is known as Puspadanta, a staunch devotee of Siva. He gained the capacity to become invisible at will and used this invisibility to steal flowers from the king's garden to give to Lord Siva. In order to catch the thief of flowers, the king scattered the flowers taken off from the idol of the Lord in the hope that the thief would lose his capacity to disappear by treading on these flowers. Puspadanta trod on the flowers unknowingly, and lost his power of invisibility. In order to regain that lost power he composed this hymn to please the Lord. Text in English and Hindi.

65 pages. Paperback.

US $3.50 Item No. 52. Shipping: $0.50

THE MESSAGE OF BUDDHA
A. S. Wadia

What is the secret of Buddhism's influence on the mind and the imagination of humanity for over two thousand years? Does it awaken some long-neglected chord of the human heart? Does it touch some secret spring deep in the depths of the human soul? This volume brings together the ideas and tenets of Buddhism, interpreting them in the light of the fundamental principles of human life as well as in the light of the latest science of the human mind.

238 pages. Hardback.
US $6.40   Item No: 81 7303 000 6 Shipping: $1.00

ORACLES AND DEMONS OF TIBET: THE CULT AND ICONOGRAPHY OF THE TIBETAN PROTECTIVE DEITIES
Rene de Nebesky-Wojkowitz

This book is a study of the Tibetan protective deities, those gods worshipped by the Tibetans as protectors and guardians of Buddhism. It details the classification, appearance and attributes of these gods (their iconography) and how they are worshipped through sacrifices, offerings, ceremonies, oracles, feasts, prophetic trances, ritual dances, black magic and weathermaking (their cult). "Monumental piece of research"—The Independent (Kathmandu).

666 pages. Paperback. B&W plates, diagrams.
US $19.25   Item No: 81 7303 039 1 Shipping: $2.00

CENTRAL ASIA AND TIBET
Sven Hedin

In 1899 the famous Swedish explorer, Sven Hedin, set out on one of his most hazardous journeys: to visit the little known interiors of Central Asia and Tibet. A three year voyage ensued amidst remote peoples and through inhospitable terrain. Hedin's goal was to penetrate the then forbidden city of Lhasa...but the Tibetans had other ideas!

2 volumes. 608 & 664 pages. Hardback. B&W plates & photographs; foldout colour maps.
US $48.00   Item No: 81851321143 (set) Shipping: $3.50

THE DHAMMA-CAKKA-PAVATTANA SUTTA
translated by Sister Vajira
A classic reprint of the Buddha's first sermon delivered at Sarnath, India. English text with Pali transliteration. Originally published by the Maha Bodhi Society at Sarnath.
35 pages. Pamphlet.
US $1.95 Item No. 47. Shipping: $0.50

AVADHUTA GITA OF DATTATREYA
Dattatreya
This work by the great yogi Dattatreya expounds Hindu philosophy in a bold and subtle analysis. An introduction to the work and a biography of the author are included.
90 pages. Paperback. Printed on art paper.
US $5.00 Item No: 020 Shipping: Sea $ 0.50

A CONQUEST OF TIBET
Sven Hedin
Sven Hedin, adventurer, in the unknown land of Tibet: among Mongols and robbers, in disguise towards Lhasa; prisoner of Kamba Bombo; in the home of the nomads; in mysterious monasteries...Non-stop excitement in an exotic locale. "Fascinating tale of adventure, discovery and hairbreadth escapes"—New York Times. "Exquisite imagery"—Christian Science Monitor.
400 pages. Hardback. Line drawings.
US $16.00 Item No: 81 7303 016 2 Shipping: $1.50

THREE YEARS IN TIBET
by Ekai Kawaguchi
A classic reprint of a Japanese monk's spiritual odyssey, recounting his journey to Tibet from Japan in 1897. In his quest to study Tibetan Buddhism and language, the author travelled in disguise throughout Tibet staying at monasteries as he sought out the wisdom of ancient texts and their hidden meanings. Differing from western accounts, Kawaguchi describes Tibet from the point of view of an Asian intimately acquainted with its manners and customs.
719 pages. Paperback/Hardback. B&W illustrations.
US $19.50/$21.25 Item No. 81-7303-036-7 Shipping: $2.50

MUSTANG: A LOST TIBETAN KINGDOM

Michel Peissel
The kingdom of Mustang lies hidden in the Himalayas of northern Nepal. Foreigners were forbidden to travel to Mustang and little was known about its people and civilisation until Michel Peissel made his journey there in 1964. He found a medieval world preserved from modern technology, in which the wheel was not used, the earth was believed to be flat and polyandry practised; but a land with beauty and happiness in spite of hardships. "Real treat for the armchair traveler" — New York Times Book Review.
288 pages. B&W and colour photographs.
US $14.40 (Hardback)   Item No: 81 7303 002 2
US $12.00 (Paperback)   Item No: 81 7303 008 1
Shipping: $1.00

LOST IN THE HIMALAYAS

by James Scott and Joanne Robertson
The incredible story of how the Aussie trekker survived 43 days in the Himalayan winter without food or shelter. Fighting cold, hunger, isolation and despair, James tells his story of how he got lost—and rescued in the high Himalayas of Nepal. It is also the story of another struggle—that of his sister Joanne and how she too refused to give up hope to find James alive. An inspiring story about hope, endurance, survival and the human spirit. Foreword by Tim Macartney-Snape.
197 pages. Paperback. B/W photos and illustrations.
US $13.75 Item No. 81-7303-030-8 Shipping:$1.50

PEAKS AND LAMAS

by Marco Pallis
A classic reprint of a spiritual journey through the Himalayas of then British India and Tibet in the 1930s. Along the course of this in-depth journey, the author discovers the Lama—the guide whose hand sustains the climber as he strives to reach the summit of enlightenment, and his realization of the Lama as the Universal Teacher.
428 pages. Hardback. B/W photographs, illustrations and period maps.
US $19.75 Item No. 81-7303-013-8. Shipping: $2.75

CONFESSION

by Kavita Ram Shrestha. Translated by Larry Hartsell.
Controversial and boldly written, this powerful translation is available for the first time in the English language. The Nepali characters of a sick woman, a dwarf and a whore portray frustrated people which society creates but then turns into objects of hatred. Although it is a story of opposition to society's values, it is, as the author says, "a story that exists in all places, times and personalities." Introduction by Krishnachandra Singh.
US $3.75 *75 pages. Paperback.*
Item No. 81-7303-033-2. Shipping: $0.75

BENDING BAMBOO: CHANGING WINDS

by Eva Kipp
In modern Nepalese society many changes influencing women are taking place. From personal stories and interviews of women representing varied ethnic groups and castes found in Nepal, this impressive book dramatically captures what village women think about the different aspects of their lives and the changes that are taking place. The stories and beautiful photographs reveal a wealth of information and a rare glimpse into the thoughts, beliefs, worries and pleasures of Nepali women today. With contributions from: Kim Hudson, Lucia de Vries, Marieke van Vliet and Alieke Barmentloo.
161 pages. Paperback. Printed on art paper. Colour photographs.
US $14.95 Item No. 81-7303-037-5. Shipping: $1.50

(All shipping rates quoted are for sea mail. Postage and handling for air mail is eight times sea mail rate for each book. For larger orders, please write, fax or e-mail.)

These and other fine titles may be ordered directly from our distributors. Personal bank drafts drawn off any major currency accepted by post and credit card orders accepted by fax with card number, expiration date and signature. Request our free publication catalogue.

PILGRIMS BOOK HOUSE
P.O. Box 3872, Kathmandu, Nepal
Fax: 977-1-424943. E-mail: info@pilgrims.wlink.com.np
Web Site: http://gfas.com/pilgrims

EIC